Love, Lies

&

Temptation

Denecia Green

Love, Lies & Temptation

Published by Denecia Green

Copyright©2017 by Denecia Green

ISBN: 978-1-949343-17-5

Dedication

This book is dedicated to the memory of my grandmother, the late Vivia Dorene Stewart, whose unfailing love and kind words continue to define me and keep me grounded throughout my life. She kissed all my fears and insecurities away and her gentle breeze has often kept my sails filled with the wind of destiny.

Acknowledgement

I am deeply grateful to God for the gifts He has allowed this journey to bring into my life. He has blessed me in spite of myself, and I am humbled by His grace.

To my family, thanks for your undying love, support and encouragement to follow my dreams; your kind words and gentle nudges catapulted me to new heights.

Many thanks to Ms. Stacey A Palmer, my editor, for your listening ear and literary suggestions that thickened the plot and made my words come to life. To Jonathan Cooke, you are a talented Web designer and Jamie Barnett, a very skilled photographer. Thank you both for creating such an aesthetically pleasing cover.

To my readers, thank you so much for the never ending support you have shown me. You could have done many other things with your hard earned dollars; I am appreciative that you chose to purchase this book; and I hope that you enjoy it.

Also by Denecia Green

Life: Through A Teen's Eyes

A compilation of short stories capturing the life of typical modern teenagers from various socioeconomic backgrounds. The range of stories cover light hearted experiences such as the first kiss, the power of generosity as well as more heavy-set experiences, including dealing with death, abuse and drug addiction. The stories are intended to inspire and guide readers on how to deal with a few challenges of life.

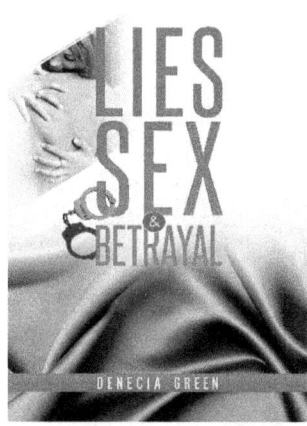

Lies, Sex & Betrayal

In weaving a tapestry of Jamaican life predicted on a get-rich -quick scheme and illegal drug use. Lies, Sex & Betrayal offers an inside look of life on the wild side with chilling intimacy. Kim, the dollar-hungry entrepreneur with her raging thirst for sex, handled her business by any means necessary after her lover; a drug kingpin was placed behind bars. Briana whose main foci were her man and success, was shocked out of her comfort zone after meeting Alex.

Both women were forced to face their secret and desires. Lies, Sex & Betrayal is a steamy story with all the plot twists one craves in matters of the heart.

1

Briana

I love my life. I love my job. I love my friends. I love my house. I love my charity organization, and I love my car. Oh, did I say I love my life? Well if I didn't. I love my life. I really love my life.

I stepped out of my shiny red Honda Civic, then opened the passenger door and picked up four trays of catered food lying on the seat. I had about 40 minutes before the girls would be over for our usual weekend flex. All I had to do was arrange the food and have a quick shower. The food was easy-thanks to the supermarket/deli store that was a few blocks away from where I lived. I merely had to remove the tops from the trays of the barbeque ribs, fried chicken wings, freshly prepared rice and peas which would go nicely with the macaroni and cheese and potato salad I prepared earlier. To add the finishing touch, I needed to pull out a few bottles of wine from my stash and voila, dinner is served.

I entered my house and placed the food on the island in the kitchen then looked around the room with admiration. I was proud of myself. I had been living in my town house for about a year, and I still couldn't believe how beautiful it was. My kitchen had black granite countertops, stainless steel appliances and handcrafted cherry wood cabinets. The designs for the kitchen I copied from a home remodeling magazine turned out more beautifully than I had imagined, and so did the rest of my house. God, I do love my life. The only thing missing was a man to share it with, but then that was a minor factor-or so I convinced myself. I was content with the way things were. I headed down the hall to the room I called my sanctuary-mainly because of the state of the art home theatre system I recently had installed, which was aptly complemented with over nine hundred DirecTV channels. I was in fifty- two inch plasma television heaven. I straightened the chaise lounge chairs and made sure everything was in place for whatever activities the girls agreed to. I hurriedly made my way to the bathroom and quickly showered. I got dressed just as quickly, then reapplied my makeup.

A few minutes later, the doorbell rang. My first thought was that it was probably Melonie. She was always on time. This woman had never been late for anything. Kim, on the other hand, was the complete opposite; she was always fashionably late, unless there was something monetary to be gained. The way to Kim's heart was money; she was my dollar hungry entrepreneur friend who I loved dearly. I went up front to answer the door and as expected, it was Melonie. Hot to Trot, Melonie showed up wearing an all-red form fitting outfit I wouldn't have been caught dead in. I know I sound like I am hating, but that's because I am. I couldn't stand the tight shit she wore, but the thing I hated most about her outfits was that she actually looked cute in them. Her overly attractive face and curvy figure made her look drop dead gorgeous, no matter what she wore. It's not that I looked bad. Hell, you couldn't tell me I wasn't beautiful. Plus, I could dress my ass off too but truth be told, I think I was slightly jealous of her, because I noticed Alex fishing around the office occasionally, the way he did when he spotted his next target. Physically, she had what appealed to him, so there was a strong possibility. It's not like I would ever go back to Alex, so I am not even sure why it made me slightly jealous seeing them together. Putting those factors aside, she was a really nice person and a great coworker.

Five minutes later, the woman I considered to be the life of any social gathering, my very spirited and passionate, dollar-hungry friend, Kimberly, and her crazy ass friend Anastasia arrived. The minute she closed the door behind her she started yelling "Sexy ladies in the house," then cupped her ear waiting for our reply. We didn't disappoint her, as a chorus of "Sexy ladies in the house!!!" rang out in response. Kimberly made her way to the food, and didn't hesitate to make herself a plate. Melonie later joined her; meanwhile, Anastasia was stirring up everybody about an encounter she had the night before. "Hold up, I know y'all not about to get your sex talk on and we haven't even blessed the food,"

I said interrupting the moment. "Well then let's bow our heads, because this prayer will be the only Christian thing that comes out of our mouths tonight," Anastasia shot back. "The power of the vagina," Kim said devilishly right before she bowed her head to begin the prayer.

From that point, I knew it was going to be one hell of a night. "Yeah, so back to the story" Melonie said. "No, I think we should save the best for last," Kim said. "Let's start with the most boring person we know in this room," Kim continued. Then suddenly all eyes were on me. "I am not boring" I said defensively. "According to who?" they all chorused. "Have you gone out with anyone yet since Alex?" Kim asked. "It's been like..what..ten years?" she continued. I rolled my eyes. "I am working on it."

"I am sure you are. Working seven days per week is not my definition of working on it," Kim said as she tried to make me feel bad about my situation.

"She may be man less but her crib is the shit," Anastasia blurted out.

"True, true" they all agreed. "These ribs are everything too!" Melonie added. "Did you make these?" Kim shot Melonie a sarcastic look then added "you know better than to ask that," I threw a perfectly good chicken wing at Kimberly in protest to her remark. Feeling a little flushed by being the main topic, I deviated the conversation to Anastasia.

"Now can we get back to the juicy story?" I said as I poured four glasses of wine.

"Ok, so I went out with this guy the other night," she began. "I loved his company. Dinner went well, so I decided to speed things up and basically offered a blow job".

"On the first date?" I interjected.

"Shhhhhh" they all chorused.

"Yeah so anyway, he practically turned me down. I figured he probably had some really horrifying encounter, because I am yet to meet a man who refuses a blow job. I told him how much I wanted to show him my skills even in my most sultry voice, and the man still said no. So of course, this dampened my spirit a little bit. But then he told me it was just not his thing and that he just wanted to be inside of me. That sexy whisper in my ear immediately got my juices flowing." We all laughed in unison. She continued, "so we started kissing passionately, and he led me to his bedroom where he turned off all the lights.

"Sumn aint right with this nigga," Kim blurted out.

"Roger that" Melonie added. I sat anxiously trying to wrap my mind around her story.

"He even closed the blinds in the bedroom after turning off all the lights. I tried to protest but then he

11

was between my legs so fast, licking and sucking me to ecstasy that my mind pretty much went blank."

"So hold up!! Home boy is not into receiving head but he is into giving?" I asked. "I need one of those in my life." We all laughed, as we high fived each other in agreement. Anastasia laughed as well. "He was darn good at it too," she added. "He kissed my neck and lips, explored my breasts and eventually penetrated me missionary style. I couldn't believe how deep he was. His hardness stretching me open even wider and his hot tongue was busy with my breast. I was losing my mind. I lowered my hand to his waist but then stopped abruptly when I felt something like a belt in my hands. I playfully asked if he was wearing a belt to bed but his reaction threw me off. He became stern, pulled out of me in a hurry and jumped off the bed. I became frightened as well and jumped off the bed and opened the blinds. He was trying to grab his underwear off the floor but it was too late." Anastasia paused and sipped her wine.

"What happened?" we all blurted out. She took another sip of the wine. I grabbed the glass from her because suspense was killing me. "What the hell happened?" I asked. She laughed, almost choking on the wine. "I saw the one thing, he didn't want me to. The one thing I could never have imagined I would be seeing. The thing I felt was a belt all right. But it was the kind of belt that was holding up the big fake ass dick hanging between his legs and the bastard had the nerve to have a condom on it."

"What the friggggg?" we all chorused. I refilled her glass and handed it back to her. "Why would he need a strap on?" Melonie asked. We were all confused. "Unless you were sleeping with a transgender," I said

"Or his penis was chopped off" Kim quickly added. We all threw a chicken bone at her. Kim was always being silly. "No but seriously though Nas, was he a she?" Kim asked. "I don't even know. I left his house so fast and I haven't contacted him since. I was so embarrassed."

"But let's just back up a bit, you said you felt the plastic dick grew hard in you?" I asked dying with laughter.

"Not to mention how deep he was," Kim added. We all laughed even harder.

"That plastic dick was thebomb.com" Melonie added. By this time we were all in tears. This was too funny. "But on a serious note though, do dildos really feel like the real deal. I mean, he had a condom on it and all but still...there must have been some difference," I said looking at both Kim and Anastasia for some type of support or response.

"Why are you looking at me?" Kim asked. "Weh yuh know bout mi?" she continued. We all laughed. I got up and fixed myself and the girls another plate. The stories continued. It became obvious that it was going to be one hell of a girl's night indeed.

2

Kim

I peered into the ceiling and really began to assess my life. Briana was my friend but sometimes I was slightly jealous of her. It's not that I hated her or anything like that. The truth is, I admired her and wanted to be like her. She seemed to have her life all figured out. She has a nice house to host all our lovely girls gathering; plus, she is single and doesn't seem to be bothered by that fact. Even though I tease her about it, I really don't want her to compromise her standards and settle for less than what she deserves. I may get jealous occasionally, but I still want the best for her. I, on the other hand, am still fighting to carve my path in this life. I am yet to discover my true sense of purpose. I refuse to accept that the life I have now, is all that is in store for me. I am nowhere near my maximum potential, and I will never stop fighting until I truly feel that I am.

My life is not as bad as I make it seem, but I am just not living the lavish life that I yearn for. I suppose I am still grateful for what I have, because I am still able to make ends meet. I have a start-up business at home where I host an event where I prepare and serve fried chicken wings on Fridays; the event is themed "Wings & Drinks." Thus far, the event has been well-supported, and I am happy for this, especially since it hasn't been heavily promoted. I have been doing this for about one month now and to date, I have no regrets. Occasionally, I will also cater for various events endorsed by my mother's church. This was how I got my big break. There is a basic school attached to the church that is also managed by the pastor, so after introducing the members of the church to my finger licking culinary skills at their minor events, he landed me the offer of providing lunch on a daily basis to the students and staff at both the school and the church, from Mondays to Thursdays as I have to prep for my event at home on Fridays. For the most part, it warms my heart to see the kids devour their meals. Not to mention moments when they would all bombard me exclaiming how delicious their lunches tasted. Who would have thought those words would have been music to my ears? I never get tired of hearing it. I guess for me, it was a form of self-recognition. Being praised was not the only motivating factor though. Growing up, I always hated the cafeteria food. Because of this, I tried to be creative when prepping the meals. My goal is to satisfy every child's hunger; and make them look forward to their lunch break. So I guess one could say, in terms of my career, I am managing.

I was learning to satisfy with slowly making ends meet and enduring the rough patch that is occasionally associated with business adventures. I had not been in any dealings with Bugz & Anastasia. I was trying to clean up my life, letting go of the past and embracing God. I believe that God will bless abundantly those who persevere in seeking Him. I know He may not come when we want him, but I do believe He will be there right on time. Learning spiritual warfare was one of the most interesting things happening in my life to date. I never knew the house of the Lord could be so fun and soothing. All this time, I have been running from one man to the next. Now, I have come to find, so much more from a man named Jesus. A man who has always been there no matter how many times I have betrayed and persecuted him. He is still a merciful and forgiving God. My sins have mounted up against me, convicting and sentencing me to death. Yet, God defended me, stood in my place, took the blame and bore the shame for me. I am alive today because of his grace, atonement and redemption; redemption available to lowly me. He washed the blood from my hands, heard the confession, and touched me when others thought me untouchable. He healed my pain, when I thought I would lose my mind. I was angry, hurt, disappointed, grieved. But all these emotions subsided, when I simply made the choice to attend church more often. At times, I wondered if I even deserved the next breath. I sighed...closed my eyes and sighed once more then whispered a prayer.

"Thank you Jesus for your way out by acknowledging my sin, as I turn away, never to walk that way again. The way of gossip, pride, bigotry, lies, hatred. I also ask that you help me dismiss that occasional feeling of jealousy towards Briana. Thank you for the joy of release. I praise you for the opportunity to repent. Thank you for your love. My spirit and flesh submit to you, and I am glad. Order my footsteps, dearest God and lead me not into temptation but deliver me from evil, Amen.

I turned on my side, fluffed my pillow twice before peacefully drifting off to sleep.

3

Briana

Somehow, the girl's night triggered in me a bit of soul searching. The remarks about my single life replayed in my mind. Had it really been that long? I became so complacent with being single that even though years had passed, and it felt like only months to me. I don't know if I should be bothered by the fact that I was totally fine with being single. In fact, it almost felt like second nature. Some people made it look like a sin, but-I enjoyed my own company. It's so much easier and stress-free. Even so, I decided that it was time to do something about it. That means, I needed to be seen at places outside of work and my home. So I opt to utilize one of the tickets I had received for the upcoming Major Lazer & Friends Concert tonight that everyone seemed to be raving about. I seemed to be the only one out the loop but thanks to Google, I was able to I fix that right away. Kim was busy, so I had no company. Melonie was available, but I am sure Alex could buy her a ticket, if she really wanted to go. I needed a little more time to come to terms with the fact that my ex may become my coworker's future boyfriend. The thought still made me edgy, so for that petty reason, I didn't bother to request her company. Since I opted to go alone, I decided to dress in such a way that screamed, 'single, sexy and ready to mingle.' That was the only way I would have met someone to keep my company for the night. If this didn't happen within my first two hours at the venue, then I would call it quits and head home.

The day went by quickly, and in no time I was dressed and ready to party. I took a quick glance at myself in the mirror; I approved.

Upon arriving at the venue, my first mission was to sample everything from the various food stations. I kept it light because I was mindful of my belly protruding in the dress. So I fed on multiple cups of conch soup, two servings of spring rolls, and I was filled in no time. I found a little spot near the fence, but close enough that I could see everything,-that I decided to remain for a little while. This spot warranted attention but not from the type of people I imagined. I was approached mainly by men who were already intoxicated or whose breath wreaked of the combination of cigarette and cheap liquor. As soon as one person left, another one approached me. It was taking a lot out of me, to hold my breath at short intervals just to keep off the awful smoke scent coupled with trying to politely turn them down. When I couldn't take it anymore, I relocated. This time moving closer to the stage. This turned out to be even more exciting, as I was in the heart of the party. The front section had a vibe. The way in which we all sang and danced together, you would have sworn we had known each other for quite a while. I was surprised at how much of a good time I was having and ended up staying well over my proposed two hour period.

Closer to the end of the concert, that's when I gave someone my number who I thought was attractive. Although there were no real sparks, I didn't think that I had anything to lose, so I went with the universe. It doesn't hurt to get to know new people. He escorted me to the parking lot. There was- not much of a conversation on the journey, but that's only because I was drained. I really just wanted to get home. I don't even think I remembered his name, was but I figured it would eventually come up when he called.

The night turned out much better than I expected. I thanked him for the escort then drove off.

****

The next morning I slept in a bit later than usual. I did my usual routine of preparing my hot cup of coffee then relaxed in my wicker tear drop swinging chair while reading the newspaper and checking my messages intermittently. Only this time, a message from an unknown number lingered. I was curious, so I opened this message first and it read: *Hi beautiful, this is Chris. I hope you slept well?* I stared at the phone for a while as I tried to process who Chris was. Then another message read: *The guy from last night. Well maybe I should say, the one who walked you to your car just in case you had*

21

several men hitting on you since you were so stunning. I responded to his message with no real emotion then proceeded to read the paper. The nature of our conversation was basically trying to understand each other's favourite pass times, favourite meals, likes, dislikes as well as ones career- the typical getting-to-know-you conversation. He eventually called, and we were having a good conversation that unfortunately ended abruptly due to an argument ensuing among my neighbours whose details I didn't want to miss. However, we agreed to meet later at a sea food restaurant on the beach.

My community was known for drama especially from my immediate neighbours. But drama between Angella and Joseph usually happened on Sundays, so I was surprised to hear all this commotion outside today. Apparently, it wasn't a feud between the two this time but instead, an argument between Joseph and one of his baby mothers. She was arguing with him about not taking care of his child and pretty much threatened him that if she hadn't received anything by the end of the month, she would take him to court. Joseph had gotten so many women pregnant and by the look of things, he doesn't seem to be able to support them. Angella was his most recent girlfriend. A sweet young lady, might I add. I often wondered what magic words Joseph used to charm her. He didn't deserve her, but I suppose sometimes some of us find love in places and people we least expect it. This argument lasted briefly. By the look of things, it seemed like Joseph was intimidated by this particular woman because he quickly returned from the house with an envelope that I assumed contained cash. The woman took it then left shortly. I remember another woman use to visit Joseph throughout the week and quarreled with him about the same child maintenance issue, and he ignored her on every occasion. I don't know how Joseph did it because I felt drained just by watching or listening to their arguments repeatedly. But one day, the woman became frustrated and threw the child over the wall and into Joseph's house. The screams of the child caused Joseph to rush out, and that was the first time that woman received his attention. To date, I am still not sure if the child sustained any injuries.

I finished my coffee and had a French toast. This should have been enough to sustain me until I met up with Chris. Soon I was ready for my date, appropriately dressed in jeans shorts with a crop top and flip flops.

****

By the time we arrived at the restaurant, it was already buzzing with activities. They had a resident disc jockey who had clearly built up a vibe among the customers, since most persons could be seen following the dancing instructions of the disc jock. Chris and I placed our orders then headed outside to watch the beach activities. There was an interesting game of musical chairs in the form of a scavenger hunt happening which we both found intriguing. This was followed by a game of volleyball and by this time our food was ready. We ordered fried fish, lobster, and curried shrimp with a serving of bammy and festival. Chris seemed like he was a social butterfly. He was very easy to talk to, and we hit it off from the start. He had a great sense of humor as well. In fact, he made me laugh to the point where I was on the brink of tears. When we grew tired of talking, we hit the dance floor and danced like no one was watching. Of course, the dj further boosted the vibe until the floor became crowded. We danced to popular hits like: Cupid Shuffle, Wobble, Cha Cha slide and Electric Boogie, to name a few. We danced until we were the last ones remaining on the dance floor. We returned to our seats and what happened next left me feeling slightly embarrassed. I was so into the moment that I attempted to kiss him. He basically blocked my kiss but in a subtle way by-placing a smooch on my cheek. He then whispered that he didn't move this fast on a first date with women he was interested in seeing again. I was so embarrassed. I secretly told myself that I would never again make such a bold move. I will wait for him to do his thing. He settled the bill, then we left. The mood was definitely not the same. Though he still played it cool, I was flushed with embarrassment. Other than my little mishap, we had a beautiful first date, and I was eager for date number two.

4

Kim

I woke up the next morning with Bugz on my mind, and I wasn't sure why. I decided to give him a call to check in on him. He begged to see me. I only agreed to meet with him because I had a few hours to spare before I got ready for work. I was trying to wean myself from Bugz because of the influence he has on me but for some strange reason, I couldn't understand why I felt the need to see him so badly today. There was no way, I could be faced with withdrawal symptoms so soon. I slipped into one of my mini dresses then headed out.

The smell of a fresh batch of weed greeted me as I entered through the front door. I felt myself float for a few seconds, as I imagined the euphoria Bugz might be experiencing. That smell was everything. I haven't had a good joint in quite a while. "Lord, lead me not into temptation" I whispered before greeting Bugz with a hug. My eyes rolled over as the smell of good weed became more pronounced when I hugged him. "Oh gosh," I unexpectedly blurted out.

Bugz released me from his arms and looked at me with concern. "Is everything ok Kim?"

"Yes," I responded, stepping pass him to the living room where I made myself at home. "What have you been up to?

"Nothing I think you want to hear about." He responded.

I eyeballed the stash of weed that was neatly placed in the tray on the centre table.

"How are things with you and Anastasia?" I asked while still occasionally glancing at the stash. I don't know why I had come here knowing that I would have been tempted in such environs. Smoking weed was one of my biggest demons, and-Bugz always had the link for a good product. This made it that much more tempting, so I badly wanted to sample the stash.

"Nas and I are fine. We are doing our thing as usual. She is out shopping." He stated, as a matter of fact.

"The good old days," I said, as I reminisced for a moment on when I was the shit and lived the life of lavish.

"You know it doesn't have to be that way. I have you covered. Just let me know what you need."

"No hun. I am done with that life. In fact, I am toying with the idea of being baptized and giving this church thing a try," I said without hesitation.

"Really, is that why your eyes have been transfixed on the weed since you arrived?"

I couldn't contain the laughter. I was busted. I didn't realize that I had made it that obvious.

"Stop torturing yourself and satisfy your thirst," he said handing me the joint that screamed sexiness.

"No Bugz. I am ok."

"If you want to jump to the hardcore stuff, I have a stash of that too?"

I stared at the weed in his hands, then my eyes darted to the table then back to his hands.

"One last time for the road Kim, then I promise I won't hinder you from changing your life. This is the only time I will ask this of you. Have a joint with me, like old times?"

"Please Kim," he pleaded.

"Fine." I took the joint from him, rolled it through my fingers and examined it briefly before I took a deep inhalation. I exhaled and took another, then another which lead to several others. I threw my head back and basked in the moment. This was a beautiful feeling. I felt the tension leave my body as I took another puff.

"It's good right?"

I nodded in response to Bugz question with my eyes still tightly closed. It was too much of a beautiful feeling. I didn't want to let go of the moment just yet. I felt a hand gliding along my thighs; even that felt good.

I barely peeked through one eye to see Bugz advancing then closed them and allowed him to have his way. He caressed and lingered at my thighs for a moment before going for the familiar place. I felt my whole body twitch when he gently touched my sweet spot. I didn't want this to end. He used his tongues to play musical cords along my thighs until I felt him nibble on my underwear. I took another puff and relaxed even more. He lifted my butt slightly off the couch before pulling up my dress. He then pushed my panties to the side and ate me hungrily. The moment his lips touched my vagina, I felt it trembling even more. "Don't stop...Please don't stop." I moaned.

"Don't worry sweetie, I have been longing to do this. I missed tasting you," he murmured before driving back into my muff for another licking. His tongue darted in and out bringing me to an orgasm. That same moment we heard keys turning in the lock, but I was too spent to regain composure. My legs were wide apart exposing my goodness, but I managed to open my eyes.

Anastasia remained motionless as she tried to sum up what was happening. She closed the door behind her, dropped her shopping bags, and ripped off her clothes in record time. "I can't let you two have all the fun." Next thing I knew she buried her face between my legs. I was in heaven. Maybe not the one saints go to but this certainly wasn't hell. Anastasia with her vacuum mouth, did her signature move that had me screaming with another orgasm in a matter of second. By this point, the joint fell to the floor. I was succumbed with this raw, overly horny experience that I aggressively shoved Anastasia off me and unto floor, positioning myself in such a way, that both our vaginas touched. I eased myself off the floor and gyrated my vagina vigorously against hers. She screamed with pleasure, but this moment was interrupted by Bugz standing over her, then slowly lowered his penis into her mouth. He pounded her mouth while I pounded her with my vagina. A few minutes later, he pulled out, grabbed her off the floor and pounded her roughly until he came. Anastasia's moans resulted in yet another orgasm. I had three orgasms in less than one hour. I felt like a million dollars. I didn't linger for any form of post sex conversation. Instead, I headed home immediately where I freshened up then headed to work.

$$**********$$

I was in a superb mood at work. I hadn't had a joint that good in quite a while. I could definitely use a stash like that at home; I would have been a happy woman. It's almost as if I opened my appetite after the few puffs I took this morning. It was still as magnificent as I remembered it. Weed plus back to back mind blowing orgasm; what better way could I have started my morning. I transferred all this built-up energy into today's lunch menu. I had my usual school cafeteria duties, but then there was an impromptu members meeting by the church. The bishop asked me to prepare sandwiches for the meeting. Today, however, was his lucky day. Instead of sandwiches he requested, I opted to utilize the chicken that had been seasoned for tomorrow's lunch to prepare a meal of pineapple chicken with fried rice.

This was a quick meal, which I finished in no time. As soon as I was done, I neatly plated the meals then distributed them myself. Bishop was totally amazed by what I had done, on such short notice. I guess this earned me points in his good book. A morning initiated with amazing sex was later concluded with a flood of great reviews from all the members I catered to. Everything was fine, until bishop extended an invite for the brief prayer service he was about to have. Although I was not in the frame of mind to pray, considering my sexual escapades earlier that day, I thought it would have been rude of me to decline.

Though the euphoria associated with the weed still lingered, it wasn't strong enough to numb my emotions. Which got the best of me during the service. It's almost as if every word uttered during the service was directed at me. I could no longer hold back the tears. I knelt at the altar and cried. I poured out my heart in prayer and asked the Lord for forgiveness. On the spot, I pledged to serve Him wholeheartedly and told the persons praying with me that I was ready to be baptized but I preferred to do it in the service on Sunday.

They appeared reluctant to wait for the weekend, but-they had no choice but to accept my request. This propelled one of the members who was part of the praying group to speak with me briefly after the service. He seemed like a nice fellow. His name was Duane, and he was very handsome. I wondered if he had sexiness hidden under this loose fitting shirt and pants he wore. As he spoke, my thoughts drifted from his biblical teachings as reality crept up on me. I had three demons in this lifetime: sex, money and weed. Weed I could live without but the sex and the money, I wasn't so sure about. Was it even humanly possible for a highly sexed individual to assume the role of a nun? Becoming baptized meant no sex, no party, no more strip clubs... Holy shit!!! Was I really ready for this? I can't even imagine myself having a fulfilling life with so many crucial elements missing. No sex was like cutting off my air supply. I will need serious fasting and prayer to curb this demon. Then I found myself lusting at Duane. My eyes darted down to his feet which were so big. I immediately thought about the adage about men and big feet.

"Jesus Christ Kimberly, what is wrong with you?" I subconsciously yelled at myself. I couldn't even give this man my undivided attention for a few minutes. How was I supposed to live without a man for the rest of my life? I don't think I was being dramatic. I mean, what's the point of having a man if you can't commit sin with him? I don't know if I would ever be married. I held my head, as all these thoughts clouded my decision to walk the straight and narrow.

"Don't worry, you can't change everything all at once. The important thing is, you have decided to make the first step; which is to give your life to the Lord." His voice drew me back to the present. "Everything will work itself out and fall in place," he said reassuringly.

"Everything will fall in place", I said repeating his words. Pity he doesn't know how I wished he would fall between my legs right now. Why were my thoughts so perverted? I think my baptism needed to be in a pool of sanctified oil, because Jesus has a lot of work to do on me.

"Here is my number, feel free to call me if you need anything." He said handing me a piece of paper.

"Father God, he knows not what he is doing. Deliver him from evil Lord, because I can't promise I will call him for solely religious conversations, Amen."

5

Briana

Chris and I pretty much hit it off on our first date. Since then, we had been on several other dates and the more we courted, the more I fell for him. He occasionally did spontaneous gestures like surprising me with lunch, a bouquet or sometimes slipping an "I love you" note in my hand bag. Things were great between us. Initially, I was mad at myself for having giving up the cookie to a man within one month of dating. I felt so paranoid about the situation and basically waited for him to tell me some lame excuse as to why our relationship wouldn't work. I wasn't convinced he wouldn't have stuck with me after I had given it up so easily. But I was wrong. He still treated me like a queen. We had gotten to the point where I was comfortable with him leaving a few change of clothes for work seeing that most nights were spent with me. I really appreciated Chris and how much of a sweetheart he could be, so as a result, sometimes I played my part in giving him the occasional surprise as well. He was particularly fond of role play in the bedroom, so I invested in quite a few sex gadgets to add that extra flavor to the bedroom activities. I created my own Pandora box. The content of my box ranged from costumes, mask, whips, oils, vibrators, butt plug, sex card games and swings to name a few. You name it, I had it. I enjoyed experimenting on him with my various gadgets.

Tonight was one of those nights that I felt spontaneous. I called him to find out how far away he was from home, then I planned accordingly. I browsed my costume collection but couldn't quite decide on one that best captured the mood I was in. This was taking me longer than the norm so I settled on just a bathrobe this time around. I walked around the room butt naked still trying to evaluate my options. I flung the bathrobe on the staircase as I made my way to the kitchen to select his favourite wine. But I was soon out of time. A few minutes later, the alarm chirped announcing his arrival. I poured him a glass of red wine and threw on the bath robe. I waited for him at the top of the stairs with wine in hand.

"Hi baby," he said with a smile. "What are we celebrating?" he asked closing the door behind him.

"I like to think of it, as acknowledging good times." I approached him and gave him a succulent kiss. I took his bag then handed him the glass of wine.

"I could definitely come home to this every day." He sipped his wine while simultaneously eyeing me lustfully from head to toes.

"Are you hungry sweety?"

"Most definitely but not for food." The devilish look in his eyes resulted in juices trickling down my thighs. I rubbed his hand along my thighs just so he could feel what he had done to me. He moved it all the way up to my sweet spot and flicked his fingers a few times in my wetness. This drove him crazy. He quickly removed the glass from my hands and placed it on the counter. He took one more sip from his wine before leading me to the bedroom. "How about you let me prep you properly?"

"Whatever you want baby, I am all yours." He loosened the first three buttons on his shirt as he sat on the bed. I gently lifted each leg and took off his shoes then unbuckled his pants. He stood up and let them drop to the floor. I pulled down his boxers then went to work. I eased up for a moment not long after I started, because I was having a hard time interpreting Chris's body language. He was moaning so loudly and his movement gave me the impression that he was about to climax, but I am thinking he could not have been to that point so soon. I have never had that issue with him before but I don't know, maybe my technique had been upped a notch, so it made him even more excited than he had ever been. Not soon after I dismissed the thoughts, and resumed the blowjob that his screams resumed only this time, it was louder than before. I wasn't chancing it at all. My gut told me to get in and get my fix before it was too late. I was too wet, to not even be penetrated for a few seconds. I took off his shirt and climbed onto his lap.

When I straddled him, he grabbed my hips and pulled me closer, and in no time, I was sliding up and down his pole, grinding as I fell onto his lap. As I increased the pace, so did his moans. Usually, I was the noisy one, but Chris became the noise champion on this occasion. He had me feeling good. I slowed the pace and rocked my hips slowly, as I made my first attempt at this booty clap move I had been practicing on my pillow. I guess it was successful, because the screams now turned into curse words. I grabbed his head and looked him dead in the eyes and quickened the pace. Now this time, I was positive that he would have exploded. I watched as the veins in his forehead stood at attention, while his eyes look like they were about to plop out of socket. I bounced even harder and about five booty claps later, he gave me one last, deep thrust before falling on his back, with arms outstretched while gasping for air. I rolled off him then nestled myself under his arms. A few seconds later, he was out like a light.

I took up my phone and scrolled through the messages only to see one from Kim that which nearly gave me a heart attack. It read: *I will be baptized this Sunday, and you need to be there.*

Nothing in that sentence made sense. I knew she attended church with her mom occasionally, but I didn't know things were that serious. My Kimberly getting baptized? I wasn't sure how to react. I read the text message about three more times just to ensure that I didn't misunderstand anything, before I finally responded. I wondered what triggered the spontaneous change of heart, but I didn't bother to ask. I didn't feel like now was the right time to interrogate her. Furthermore, I didn't want it to seem like I was trying to deter her from her decision. As much as I wasn't really a fan of the church, this was a big moment for her and I wouldn't dare miss it.

I got up, showered, then carried out my nightly routine of checking to see that all lights and devices had been turned off before I armed the house. Chris didn't even bother to shower. He re positioned himself on the bed then at the wink of the eye, he was off to la la land once more.

****

I woke up early that morning and prepared a heavy breakfast of boiled dumplings, bananas with cabbage and salt fish for Chris to have before leaving for work. Whenever he overnight at my place that was usually the only time I would fix a proper meal. Otherwise, a typical breakfast for me would have been coffee with French toast and a bowl of fruits or sometimes I would only have a protein shake and I was good to go. I don't usually have an appetite in the mornings. After I sent him off with hugs and kisses, I sat on the car porch and enjoyed what appeared to be a beautiful morning. I still had a few hours to spare before getting ready for work. With my large mug of coffee in hand, I nestled my body in my wicker tear drop swinging chair and basked in the tranquility of the morning, as I breathed the fresh crisp air.

It wasn't long before my train of thoughts were interrupted by yelling from my neighbours. Their quarrels were now becoming routine. They were known for drama, which included financial, domestic or even a physical dispute. You name it; they delivered it.

"Why didn't you answer your phone woman? Didn't you see numerous missed calls from me?" Joseph scoffed as he trailed Angella and watched her empty the trash.

"Yes I did but I just needed some space and a bit of alone time to clear my mind", she said as she removed the lid from the trash can.

"Alone time and space?" he said, his voice taking on a sinister quality. " Yuh tek big man fi fool, bout alone time. Yuh tink yuh a guh have man pon di side and get weh wid it, nasty gyal Angella." The look on her face said that she was completely surprised by Joseph's behavior. But what happened next took me by surprise. He lunged towards her and snatched her in a choke hold. I was so frightened, I jolted in the chair, spilling my coffee and almost burnt myself. I always listened to them quarrel most mornings, but I had never seen their fights turn physical before-not publicly. At least, if it did, it was behind closed doors. Angella was totally unprepared for that attack. The pile of garbage fell from her hands, and she had no time to react because joseph quickly released the choke hold then placed her arms behind her. He gripped and held them firmly in place with his massive hands. With the other hand, he reached up under her dress and tried to pull down her underwear. I wondered if this their idea of foreplay and I was about to witness one of those rough sex scenes unfold or if they were genuinely having a quarrel because Joseph's actions were misleading.

His anger seemed to have magnified his strength to super human levels. I was terrified. Angella seemed powerless and terrified as well. I watched as tears streamed down her face.

"You lying, cheating, whore; just wait" By this point, his voice was so loud, I am sure all the other neighbours were watching or listening to the drama unfold. Angella stood there with her undies lying around her knees.

"Joseph stop, please stop. Let me go!" she pleaded. But he ignored her pleas and continued to rant about how he intended to prove that her reason for not taking his calls was because she slept with another man.

"You think I don't know how sex smells, you little whore. You are so nasty." He tugged at her underwear again, struggling to pull them below her knees without losing that firm grip he had on her arms.

"Let me go" she yelled as she struggled to loosen his grip on her wrists. "If you want my panties, I can give them to you dammit. Just let me go. You are embarrassing me.

"I will take them off myself. I don't need your help". And with those words, he pulled so hard that the panties came off with a loud tearing sound. He waved them triumphantly in the air as if he had just attained a major accomplishment that he loosened his grip and Angella managed to free herself.

"You are sick. Give me my darn panties." She yelled, reaching out to snatch them from him. As soon as she finally had a grip on the underwear, Joseph's raised hands came down, smashing her jaw so hard that her head snapped backwards. I gasped for air at the sight of this. She remained still on the floor for a few seconds then mumbled something after she recovered from the shock. I am not sure what was said but next thing I knew Joseph suddenly became apologetic. He knelt beside her, hugged her and must have said I am sorry about ten times. He then broke down, sobbing like a baby.

"I am so sorry hun, I didn't mean to hurt you." He continued, "I don't know what came over me. I keep picturing you with another man. It makes me crazy to think that you may go somewhere else for something I can't give you or that you may be tired of what I have to offer you. But no one else can have you hun. I love you too much. Don't you know I am crazy about you?"

Angella looked up at him with one hand clutching her injured jaw and the tears flowed down her face even more. I felt sorry for her. To my disbelief, she hugged him and it seemed like she accepted his blubbering apology. They stood up together then walked into the house arm in arm. I was still flabbergasted. My gaze was fixed outside even after they left. I guess I was trying to understand what exactly I had just witnessed. This was one of the many reasons I refrained from attempting to quell domestic disputes. They seem to have a mutually understanding relationship that on- lookers like myself failed to comprehend.

<u>6</u>

Kim

Though I had my many concerns about being baptized, I still felt slightly excited about it. I could hardly wait to share the good news with my mother. I blurted it out the moment I opened the front door. She screamed then ran towards me and gave me a hug. This was the second time, I felt like I made my mother proud. I treasured moments like these. My mom was not really a "hugger" either, so you know I felt like a million dollars whenever she responded in such manner. Her hugs were then followed by tears, but I knew they were tears of joy. Mom said a brief prayer for me before releasing me from her grasp. I called Bugz and shared the good news, but he didn't sound too intrigued by it. Considering what had transpired earlier with us basking in the euphoria of multiple orgasms, his response was totally understandable. He had a hard time grasping the sudden change of heart. I think he was more torn by the fact that I stimulated him, was able to fulfill all his fantasies and was about to end abruptly. But I blame myself; I should have never reintroduced him to something like that but then all my weaknesses were available in one place-everything was hard to resist, and that joint was so good. He remained quiet for most of the conversation but promised to attend church this Sunday to support me.

I called Duane immediately after ending the conversation with Bugz. Seeing that I should still be relatively fresh in his memory, I wanted to make a lasting impression. I was hesitant because I thought our conversation would have been strictly biblical; surprisingly, it was everything but that. I liked him even more. He seemed so humble and sweet but then only time would tell. If I didn't know anything else, I knew that people eventually reveal their true personalities. We chatted for hours. At the end of our conversation, I didn't feel like life would have been as horrible as I thought, walking the Christian faith. For that reason, I think I will keep Duane close. I felt strongly that his presence would provide the needed balance, considering the many weaknesses that I had. I was certain that Duane and Briana were the two who were sure to help me on this new journey.

Although Briana wasn't saved, she knew what she was about, and I knew she would never lead me astray. Speaking of Briana, I hadn't yet shared the news with her. Even though it was late, I decided to text her since we both had no time constraints on when we communicated. I stayed close to the phone, as I was eager to see her response but she didn't. I guess she was probably appalled by the message too.

I didn't think any more into it. Duane told me that to get familiar with the Bible I could start by reading the book of psalms, so I read the first four chapters before retiring to bed.

7

Briana

Today marked a very bitter-sweet day for me; it was Kim's baptism. I was happy that she decided to take a different approach with her life and that she seemed very passionate about it, - but I guess the thought of a new beginning for her scared me. This was so because I knew our relationship would have been somewhat affected due to her new beliefs. Most times, the things we did to unwind was definitely unacceptable according to biblical standards. I knew there were many other things we could engage in and still be able to enjoy each other's company but when you have gotten accustomed to a particular routine, it was hard to just leave it behind like it never existed; bad habits were hard to break. But I hoped and prayed that we would both be able to find the necessary will power to make our friendship work amidst her conversion. Most importantly, I secretly hoped that she didn't transform into one of those persons who acted as if they were holier than thou, finding faults with-and criticizing everyone and everything. I absolutely despised that. I believe that once a person decides to follow Christ, that he/she should be molded into a more beautiful individual if he/she is ardent about worship. After all, the Bible says, 'by their fruits you shall know them'.

This day was also interesting, because I have not been to church in ages. Church was no longer on my agenda, after I witnessed Brother Mario raping a teenager in front of my fragile teenage eyes; this experience scarred me, fundamentally. Since then, I distanced myself from everything church--related. I know that in all things you have "good fruits and bad fruits," but sometimes the "good fruits" have to pay the price for the unscrupulous ways of the "bad fruits." Although this is something that I experienced only once, it traumatized me. What compounded that experience for me is the extent to which the media had been consistently plagued with stories about pastors or some form of religious leader being charged for carnal abuse or being caught in compromising positions with ladies other than their wives; and in some cases underage girls. For me, this was disgusting and frightening. The church became a questionable organization in my eyes. The church was in shambles. No one has ever gotten me to go back to that place until this day. Kim is lucky I love her.

I smoothed out my vintage pleated skirt then added a finishing touch to my face, when my cell phone rang. I wasn't even given a chance to answer when Kim started yelling at me. "Briana, did you forget my baptism is today? The sermon will be delivered soon and you are not here yet."

That was perfect I thought. I was doing good time then. I was not trying to sit in a church from start to finish. I would arrive just in time to hear the message then watch the baptism. "I am on my way," I said and ended the call. I grabbed my car keys and headed out.

I arrived at the church in approximately twenty minutes, fashionably late. The message was in full swing. I spotted Kim and made my way towards her. I could feel the eyes piercing my skin. "Better late than never," I said slapping her on the thigh as I sat beside her. Anastasia and Bugz were also present. She had the support of her squad. She smiled from ear to ear then held my hand. She seemed so happy, and it made me happy that she was happy. I scrutinized my environment before focusing on the message being delivered.

"Many see Jesus as a way to heaven and the solution to spiritual problems, but they fail to see that He is the solution to all of life's problems. I'm addressing the emotional baggage that keeps us from total health. You can't expect the human race to move over because you had a bad childhood." And with just those two last words uttered by the pastor, I was flipped into the past.

"If you scream, I will kill you." I heard those cold menacing words coming from brother Mario. He then pushed her legs apart and thrust into her. Alicia screamed and he thrust even harder and she screamed and pleaded for him to stop." I removed my hands from Kim's grip and held my head with my eyes closed. I

fought hard to block out the memories. *"Take control Lord,"* I whispered. *"Let Go Briana...Let go"*. Kim's gentle touch on my legs brought me back to reality.

"Are you ok?" she whispered.

"I will be. I will tell you later." I answered. Channeling my energy back to the sermon.

The pastor reminded the congregation of the importance of releasing bitterness and pain. He stressed a person's attitude affected their situation. "The problem is not how much you have, but what you do with what you have", he said with great emphasis and a long pregnant pause. You could tell by how quiet the church was that everyone, even the Choristers and I, was in deep introspection and reflection about their own lives.

You could tell that the preacher was moved and operating with the motivation of a higher being. He continued with his sermon by reminding the congregation that fixing circumstances was like applying a band aid but that healing attitudes was the only thing that would truly set people free to receive the wholeness of God's blessing.

"Don't expect God to heal the superficial of who you are; He is a mighty God, so He will also heal your emotions. He may not do it in the time you expect, but He WILL heal you."

"Amen," said the church in unison.

"James 4 VS 10 reminds us to humble ourselves before the Lord, and He will exalt us. In Luke 13 Jesus cured the woman who was crippled for 18 years. The woman's twisted body symbolizes people who lack hope, or see only the negatives. With Jesus' help, we can be hopeful in God. To the persons who are supposed to be baptized shortly, you have to be resolute in worshipping God. The moment you are placed in that body of water and made anew, the enemy will attack. Be prepared, because you will be in for a fight. We are not perfect and we all falter at some point, but never let your faith dwindle. Put on the whole armor of Christ and remain resolute."

As the sermon got to its crescendo, the choristers and all the goodly Christians-nodded, clapped and blurted the occasional amen. My one regret after hearing that beautiful and timely sermon, was that I had not heard it from the beginning. It was a great one, and very timely, especially in light of Kim's decision. Kim left us and went to prep for her baptism.

"Is there anyone here who feels like they are ready to turn a new page and give their life to the Lord?" Is there anyone here, who needs us to pray with them?" The pastor waited a few minutes, but the altar remained empty. "Don't be afraid to come to the altar. We will just pray for you. Maybe you have been bound by a particular situation in your life or you may feel like you are at the point where you can't handle any more of anything bad or negative-like you are at the end of your rope. Come; let us pray for you."

The choristers then began singing "Create in me a clean heart," then one by one persons approached the altar, Anastasia and Bugz included. Bugz stood out like a sore thumb, because of his thug-like attire. His jeans pants was positioned under his ass instead of on his waist, revealing his under garment. This was paired with a t-shirt and sneakers. Anastasia, on the other hand, was more appropriately clad. Notwithstanding, they were at the altar. I, however, remained seated and bowed my head in prayer.

When the altar call ended, it was time for the moment we had all been waiting for. I walked up to the front of the church, and was granted permission to position myself on the rostrum and take photographs. Anastasia stood to the left of the pool and I was to the right. Bugz just stood and watched. You could tell he was astonished by the proceedings. I knew exactly how he felt, but I was slowly accepting the fact that this moment meant a whole new reality for me. I cued the video, to capture the exact moment she entered the pool. She was dressed in a white overall. The pastor said many things, but I only started to pay attention when I heard him say "I now baptize you in the name of the father, the son and the holy ghost..." Kim was then pulled backwards and under water for a few seconds and as soon as she came up, everyone rejoiced. I was overwhelmed with emotions. My Kimmy had been baptized; the official new beginning.

8

Kim

I felt refreshed and excited to begin this new chapter of my life. I felt like a burden had suddenly been lifted. After my baptism, I was greeted by numerous members of the church offering me congratulatory messages and well wishes on my new journey. Of all my well-wishers, I knew that my mother was the happiest of everyone, because all her life she yearned for this moment for me. I must admit that growing up I caused her a lot of heartache; I was quite the challenge for her to raise. I didn't take heed to any of her warnings. Even after I moved out, she continued to guide and pray for me, and I would shut her down. Then when I hit rock bottom with my ex, I had nowhere else to go, so I went back home and she welcomed me with open arms. I have turned my back on my mother so many times, but she still loved me and believed in me. Apart from this moment, I knew she was also proud of the job I landed cooking for the church and being able to start a business for myself at home. I was grateful for everything and especially grateful for the second chance I was given to write my wrongs. Now that I had Jesus in my life, I was looking forward to achieving greater things.

I was also grateful that my friends took the time out to be present at my baptism; although Briana was extremely late, she didn't miss my big moment. It was a great day indeed.

After all the excitement at church ended, my friends all headed to my house. My mom immediately prepped Sunday dinner. Luckily, I had some wings left over from Friday in addition to a bag of fries, so I prepared that and served to my guests. Bread was also offered as an alternative to the chips and everyone was cool with that. Everyone was famished, so my leftovers did the job. As we ate, Briana and Anastasia showed me the pictures and videos from the baptism; I am glad they captured the moment.

"Thanks again for coming guys; I really appreciated it."

"Anything for my baby girl", Bugz said pulling out a joint then pausing for a few seconds after catching up with himself. "Am I allowed to smoke around you?"

I smiled. The fact that he was concerned about smoking in my presence proved that he respected me and what he deemed to be my new beliefs. "Yes you may," I finally answered.

"Are you sure babe?" he asked again.

"Yes I am sure, Bugz"

He lit up his joint, easing back and relaxing a bit more in the chair. That joint smelt as good as the one he gave me a few days ago. Just the sight of it made me twitch. Bugz always had the good stash. I yearned for another one. I could feel myself lift as I reminisced on it being placed between my lips. I should not have given him permission, because the smell of it was doing things to me but I tried my best to ignore it. Also, I didn't want to be enforcing rules so soon. The last thing I wanted was my friends to think I immediately transformed into miss goody two shoes.

"So what happened to you in church?" I asked Bri.. Bugz and Anastasia's attention now drawn to me.

"Oh don't worry about it; it's nothing," Bri responded.

"It didn't seem like nothing to me. You seemed agitated at one point," I said staring into her eyes and secretly hoping she would tell me the truth. I sometimes hated the fact that Briana was so secretive.

"It's fine."

"Bri, can you please tell me what that was about or at least reassure me that it was nothing detrimental or nothing requiring me to put on my spiritual armor and fight." Although they all laughed at my spiritual talk, I was very serious. After all, Briana was one of my better friends.

"I just had flashbacks during the sermon about something that's all."

"Why do I always have to fight to get information from you? Sometimes I don't feel like you trust me Bri,' I responded pitifully.

"No..no..It's not like that." She released a long sigh before she spoke.

"I grew up in church as a child. But the young girls in the church would always fight for the boys' attention but at one point they desperately craved the attention of one guy in particular. He was very handsome, and he was an amazing singer. Except, this person was an adult; one of the ardent ministers in church. But you know, back then, a guy who could sing was a thing regardless of the age. So the girls in the church competed with each other for his attention until one day one of them was granted the extra attention but in a way she least expected. One Sunday, he singled out this girl and they played and flirted with each other all through Sunday school. He told her to remain after church in order to go over, the morning's lesson. That they did for a little while until the church grounds was pretty much empty. The grounds man came to lock up but he told him to give him a few more minutes. So he took the girl to the back of the church then initiated foreplay. All of which she enjoyed, while I on the other hand enjoyed the peep show. Then he beckoned for her to follow him upstairs to the office, as he had something to give her. She hesitated and the foreplay continued downstairs so that gave me time to run upstairs and position myself for the rest of the movie."

I smirked at the fact that Briana was inquisitive since she was a very good age.

She took a sip of her drink before continuing. "But then when they both entered the office and he closed the door with the keys, I sensed fear. I didn't like how this movie was playing out at all. But then when he grabbed her and covered her mouth and threatened to kill her if she screamed, that took me completely off guard. I swore I peed my pants; that's how frightened I was. He then threw her on the floor and they both fought until he finally managed to penetrate her. I watched the goodly Christian rape the teenager and when the ordeal ended, he used her stockings to wipe his penis. Then as if that wasn't enough, he went on to humiliate and abuse her verbally and mentally then had the nerve to hum a gospel song without skipping a beat as he exited the office. I was overwhelmed with emotions as I watched the sixteen year old listless on the floor with blood trickling along her thighs. I watched her clean herself and the office then wobbly exited the office. I didn't know what to do. I wanted to help, but then I quickly thought, what if I did and he raped me too. I was bothered by the fact that I hid in the closet the whole time and watched everything. It angered me that the God we served allowed such a thing to happen to an innocent girl. I was confused by how, the man we admired in the church, and who preached heart warming messages on Sundays was the same man who transformed into a rapist. Then I wondered how many others were like that. The pastor may not even be a man of God. The church was filled with hypocrisy and evil. So from that day, I stayed away. The members called me and I ignored them all. I lost all confidence in the church and I never went back until this day. So you know you are special to me because no one has ever gotten me near a church since then, not even for special events."

I couldn't help but hug her because I felt her pain. She was traumatized. I suppose any young person would be after witnessing something like that.

"Did you ever talk to someone about what you saw or even the victim?" Anastasia asked.

"No....but maybe I should have because maybe I wouldn't still be traumatized years after. I just didn't feel like I could trust anyone."

"But Bri...You can't judge the whole church because of one incident. I know it must have been frightening, but remember in everything there's good and bad. It doesn't mean that everyone who goes to church is a rapist or not a true believer." I interjected. "Remember that church is a place for broken souls. I am a perfect example. You know I am far from holy but I made a decision to let go and let God. My intention is to turn from all my dirty ways but you and I both know this won't be easy. Bad habits are hard to break. So yes, I may falter and maybe I will be judged by on-lookers like yourself because I am supposed to be living righteously but it is a hard road to travel. I am not justifying what he did but I am just saying, unfortunately sometimes people mess up. We have to learn to forgive and forget and we have to learn to bounce back if we fall short."

"I know, but it is easier said than done." Bri responded.

"I would love for you to come back to church with me one day." I said cautiously.

"I aint promising you that," she shot back without even giving it much thought.

I hugged her once more, then it dawned on me maybe that was the reason she was terribly late.

Bugz chimed in, "Briana, I hope you figure out some way to deal with that ordeal", he then got up. "This was nice, but unfortunately I have to leave now. He hugged me then whispered in my ear "don't turn into a crazy Christian now."

I laughed and punched his arm.

"But you know I am always here if you need me," he continued. He kissed me on my cheek then hugged me once more. The way he hugged me it was as if I was moving to another country. Anastasia also said her good byes then left with Bugz. Bri and I cleaned up then went inside the house to keep mom's company. A somber and celebratory mood remained the same for the rest of the evening. It's been a great day; To God be the glory, great things He has done.

****

The following morning I became very pensive. I laid in bed for a while, reminiscing on my life: The friends I have lost, the people I have met and just some of the struggles I have endured. I couldn't help but be grateful and appreciative for all the Lord has blessed me with and how much I have grown in the past few months prior to my baptism. Still, there was just something off about the way I was feeling this morning; I just wasn't able to figure out exactly what it was. Instead of worrying too much about it, I prayed about it and had a much longer devotion than I normally would especially since I was up one hour earlier than my usual time.

I picked up one of my devotional guides, written by T.D. Jakes, that my mother had given me as a gift after my baptism. I opened the cover only noticing for the first time her message inscribed to me: "Hide God's word in your heart so that you will not sin against him. Love always." I was flipping through the pages when one chapter caught my attention. It reads: *'Every Woman Needs a Sabbath'*. I read the scriptures associated with the chapter, but then I had a hard time putting things into perspective, as I tried to decide which day was rightfully considered the Sabbath day. I examined my day of worship, then I examined the other days people worshipped and read the scripture once more but to no avail. I was still clueless. The Bible has had so many different- interpretations. I skipped to another section which was much easier to understand. This subsection was entitled: YOU HAVE BEEN BENT OVER LONG ENOUGH.

"Interesting and timely", I thought.

It read: *"You have had enough tragedy. You have been bent over long enough. God will do something good in you. God kept you living through all those years of infirmity because he has something greater for you than what you have ever experienced. You may have been abused and misused. Perhaps all those you have trusted in, turned on you and broke your heart. Still, God has sustained you. You didn't make it because you were very strong. You didn't make it because you were smart. You didn't make it because you were wise. You made it because, God's amazing grace kept you and sustained you. God has more for you today than what you went through yesterday. So don't give up. Don't give in. Hold on. The blessing is on the way. I dare you to realize that you can do all things through Christ who strengthens you'* (Phillipians 4:13)

GOD"S BEST GIVES US HIS REST

The sinful things that you have fought to maintain in your life are not worth what you thought they were. I am referring to some of those things that have attached themselves to your life in which you find comfort. Some of those habits that you have come to enjoy and some of those relationships you thought gave security. They just haven't been profitable. Often, we settle for less because we didn't meet the best. But when you get the best, it gives you the power to let go of the rest.

I internalized these words before pouring out my heart in prayer. I felt like a champion after having a heart to heart talk with God. I was ready to start my day. I texted Briana a cheerful good morning message and wished her a productive day. I got dressed and headed out to run a few errands before showing up to school to prepare lunch for the kids.

9

Briana

This was my first time back at Club Levitate without Kim. It felt so weird without her especially since she was responsible for getting me hooked on what I refer to now as my little 'extra-curricular activity'. By now, I was seasoned to Club Levitate activities. In fact, the same "Candy" who creeped me out in the past with her golden showers and anal tactics was now one of my favourite dancers. Because of this, I usually tip her very well too during her sets. Kim was fascinated by her and I had grown to love her. She was very good at her job. I am not sure what today was themed as I mainly visited the club on weekends, which was always Freaky nights. I didn't feel like going home after my shift today, even though I had a hectic day. I needed some form of entertainment; so, I settled for an evening at the strip club.

It was not the usual crowd, and I arrived way earlier than my usual time. The show was in full swing regardless. On stage was a slim versus fat girls' competition among the strippers. I didn't really find this entertaining as most of the girls were basically mimicking each other's dance moves. It felt a little gimmicky and amateurish. The only thing entertaining about this segment was that the fat girls had more flesh to jiggle than their competitors. That segment was immediately followed by a stiff breast competition segment, which was dominated by the fat girls once again. After that, the girls were given a few minutes to perform their individual set. Apparently, there was a new dancer by the name of "Elastic Vagie." I didn't know her, but the audience seemed to be more than familiar as they threw a few hundred dollar bills on the stage during her introduction.

She graced the stage wearing her birthday suit, leaving nothing to the imagination and entered the stage with a container in hand. She placed the container to one end of the stage then arranged four bottles according to size, starting from the smallest. So, at the front of the line was a miniature baileys bottle, followed by half pint vodka bottle, followed by a Heineken bottle then a 341 ml Red Stripe bottle. The Dj kick started her segment with some pulsating rhythms. She danced around to the beat, bent over, and jiggled her booty while making her way towards the bottles-serenading the bottles almost. She positioned herself over the miniature Bailey's bottle then suddenly plopped down on it, consuming the bottle with her vagina. She then walked over to the container, where she hoisted one leg then literally spit the bottle out of her vagina and into the container. I then looked at the other bottles in the line, and thought that there was no way she planned to do the same thing with all the bottles because the Red Stripe bottle was too thick. To my astonishment and simultaneous delight, the same thing was done with the vodka bottle but then she changed things up when she got to the Heineken bottle. She removed the cover of the half-filled Heineken bottle, laid on the floor, spreading her legs wide open after which she inserted the bottle and emptied the contents inside her vagina. The minute she removed the bottle, she tossed the bottle aside and squirted a frothy looking liquid all over the stage while simultaneously spinning for a few seconds while she released the content from her vagina.

"Isn't she setting up herself for a yeast infection by doing that", I thought, unintentionally slipping into my medical frame of mind. But I was quickly drawn back to the stage after watching an old man use his mouth to vacuum the contents she released before placing a tip on the stage.

"Why is he not home in his bed', I thought, immediately judging the man as if I was any better. Those old bastards often time transformed into Mr. Kinky once they rolled up in the club. "I bet he wasn't licking shit like that in his bedroom", I thought, being judgmental once more.

Turning my focus back to "Elastic Vagie," only the Red Stripe beer bottle was left standing. I watched as she inverted the bottle and inserted it deep into her vagina starting from the base. I was in awe. It was now clear to me how she attained that stage name. I thought her set was over after the red stripe bottle but then she pulled out a fifth of a sour mash whiskey bottle from the container on stage and my mind wheeled. There was no way she could fit that in her vagina. That was not humanly possible. She stood in the middle of the stage making money gestures. If we wanted to see more, we had to tip. She used her tongue to play with the sprout of the bottle then occasionally caressing her clit with it and moaning while the DJ boosted the audience to tip her a little bit more. Various currencies were being thrown on the stage and the girl was motivated to proceed. I was on edge as well because I didn't think she could insert all that. A fifth of a sour mash whiskey bottle was probably like two bottles or maybe one and a half of a 341 ml red stripe bottle in terms of width. I drew closer to the stage because I had to catch every moment of this. She stretched for a few seconds before beginning her set, only this time there was no music. The entire club was silent. I watched as she slowly eased her way unto the oversized bottle. The more she lowered herself, the more the audience lowered their necks, as we all tried to monitor every inch of the bottle. She continued until the bottle disappeared. Some men climbed onto the stage, laid flat and peered right up in her vagina in disbelief. She stood still and gave everyone a chance to peek. I was curious, so I too, took a peek. I even left a tip for her as well. I couldn't believe my eyes. These women were just simply skillful. I watched her slowly as she removed it and wondered what would happen if that glass bottle should ever shatter. I don't even know why my thoughts had to stray to something like that. I guess I was just still in disbelief. I had to tell Kim about this but then I remembered, maybe she would not have had any interest in hearing this type of lewdness. By the time she removed the bottle, she jumped on the pole and danced her heart out. By this point, money rained on the stage. I guess she was the crowd favourite on a Monday night. She was not as skillful as Candy, but she could handle her business. I missed my partner in crime, but showing up to the strip club by myself turned out to be an enjoyable evening. I headed home shortly after Miss Elastic completed her set.

****

The week definitely began with a bang. Yesterday was rough, and I figured this was probably my usual Monday blues, but then by the look of things, it doesn't seem like today would have been any different. Sometimes I feel that being a certified midwife and registered nurse was the worst feat to have. It was nothing but work, especially in the public sector. Often, I did sessions in the accident and emergency unit at the hospital; and at other times, I was running from maternity wards to operating theatre. Sometimes I wondered why I even chose this profession. It was too much work. I think maybe I needed to reconsider doing more sessions in the private sector rather than public.

As I sat at the front desk of the casualty department, I was immediately greeted by Mr. UTI, a very familiar face at this hospital. I nicknamed him that because he visits here every week, religiously, for the same thing. He must have been the king of antibiotics and no matter how much I, the doctors and the pharmacist preached to him about the implications of what he was doing, he never listens. We would receive the same response about how that earned him many tips. He was a male stripper and his thing was apparently to catheterize himself and fill his bladder with wine then urinate it into women's glasses; in my opinion, very disgusting. Apparently, there are people in the world who are turned on by this. I can't see why I would want to hand over my hard-earned money for you peeing in my glass; it was ridiculous. Because we knew him very well, the doctor would write a prescription every two weeks and leave it with us at the front desk and charge him a standard fee for the month instead of for each visit. This was definitely not an acceptable thing to do, but it was a win-win situation for everyone involved. If I grew tired of seeing his face, I am sure the doc shared the same sentiment. There were a few instances where he requested to see the doctor, because-he sometimes felt that the prognosis would have been different; luckily or unluckily for him, it was always a Urinary Tract Infection. I quickly pulled up the file, filled in the date and sent him on his merry way in a matter of seconds. On several occasions, I contemplated to visit his strip club just to see how skilled he was, but dismissed the thought because I feared that he may create a scene if he recognized me. Some people tend to act up when they notice familiar faces, and I don't think I would be able to handle the additional attention; maybe I was just being paranoid about the situation.

Patient number two took the meaning of paranoid to a whole new level. The moment she sat in the chair for me to do her vitals, she questioned everything. I decided to hand her the personal information sheet to complete on her own time rather than ask the questions as I normally would. Before I knew what was happening, she was accusing me of finding out personal information to stalk her. After she completed the form, I scanned it to ensure that she didn't miss anything.

She blurted out "I wasn't beaten by a man; as a matter of fact I have never been hit by a man ok."

I ignored her and continued to scan the document. Not sure if she was trying to convince herself but I left her to have her moment.

"You people are so judgmental," she continued. *You people*, I thought. *Father God, why?? Please deliver me from this crazy woman.*

"*You* may have a seat in the waiting area and listen for your name," I told her.

"You don't hear me talking to you?" she said rudely.

"Excuse me?" I said. I swear I was ready to let this woman feel my wrath. The look on my face must have communicated that because she quickly apologized. Who would have thought she could be polite.

"I am sorry. I was just trying to practice a new move, you know, so I can shake things up a little and earn more tips," she continued. I looked at her puzzled as I tried to make sense of her ramblings.

She continued, "I am fairly new at the club but I notice most of the girls have their clientele and they are far more flexible than I was and the people loved that. Some nights my own pimp had to toss money on the stage to save me from the embarrassment. Sometimes, when you see people throwing money on the stage, we have to give it back at the end of our performance. It's just so we don't look stupid after putting on a show then not earning a dollar. So there is this girl who is the favourite. I basically tried to copy a move she did where she hooked the pole with her ass, stretching her body out so she was parallel to the floor or she would make a sudden drop face down, stopping inches away from the floor as she reached the base of the pole. This move always sent the crowd in a frenzy. So I tried it and fell right on my face. There was a lot of blood. Hence why I look like this" she sighed heavily at the end. "But you know what was amazing, as one of the bouncers helped me off the stage, I witnessed another one of the bouncers dipping his finger in the blood and tasting it. Some people have some really weird fetish, "she said.

My stomach churned at the last thing she said. I am realizing more and more that there are indeed people out there who would do extreme things. Next thing I know, the woman burst out in tears. *What the hell?* The woman's mood went from one extreme to the next in a matter of seconds.

I watched her sob for a few seconds before loosening a little. I approached her cautiously then hugged her. "You will be ok. Don't try to be like her. Just do you and get creative with it. Don't try to jump to big stunts like that; you end up hurting yourself in the long run. Now you have to stay away from the stage much longer than you bargained for with additional medical expenses. It's not worth it. Furthermore, you don't have to be skilled on the pole for people to love you. You can try doing little dance moves around the stage or perform little tricks or do some sensual dance or caressing your coworkers or something like that. Men love to see girl on girl action." I said. "Just do you," I said once more for emphasis. She looked up at me and smiled. "Were you an exotic dancer before? You seem to know your stuff," she asked.

I pretended not to hear her question and proceeded with my duties. "You may have a seat in the waiting area and listen for your name," I responded. She laughed then said thanks before leaving. "Next person for registration." I said.

I was surprised to see Alex approaching my table. "Well look who is here, the devil himself." I said greeting him.

"Ouch...that hurt."

"It's nice to be on the receiving end for once" I said, shooting him an evil glance.

"I have learned my lesson..."

"Which is what?" I asked.

"A lot of things that I would like to discuss over lunch" he responded

"That's not going to happen," I said bitterly.

"Can you hear me out please? I am begging you. Just have lunch with me once. Please...just listen to what I have to say. You don't have to say anything, just listen. It would make me feel so much better just knowing that I settled things with you properly," he pleaded.

"We have been settled. There is nothing more to discuss." I said

"Briana, please? Just this once. Have lunch or dinner with me? Please", he pleaded... "Please just think about it"

"OK I will." I said. "Thank you so much," he said smiling. "I meant ok I will think about it." I said clarifying.

"Yes I know" he said. "Still happy that you are willing to give it some thought."

I wonder if he knows that this acting pitiful stunt will not faze me. He remained still and stared at me. "Is there anything else I can help you with?" I asked.

He sighed before telling me to have a nice day. I looked him up from head to toe as he exited the building. I had not seen him in quite a while but he hadn't changed much. He just looked a little thin. Ahh well. I busied myself with paperwork at the desk glancing up at the clock every half hour. I desperately needed my lunch break. I just needed to be away from the hospital. I didn't even know where I would go; just as long as it was off the compound.

A few minutes later, Kim called asking if it was possible to have lunch that same day because she was in the vicinity. Her timing was perfect. I agreed; I was looking forward to seeing her.

With only half hour remaining to my lunch break, another patient waltzed in and plopped herself in the chair. The two girls who came with her were laughing boisterously and continuously. The woman next to me in the chair had a black eye.

"Nurse" one of the girls said laughing intermittently between sentences. "Nurse have you ever been slapped by a helicopter penis?" They all burst into laughter, even the girl with the black eye. *Helicopter penis...what the heck?* I thought. What on earth was happening at work today? The girl with the black eye continued to laugh as I attempted to register her.

"It's really nice to know that you have it in you to be laughing given your present state," I said smiling. She seemed the least bit worried about her black eye. "I know right, what a birthday gift to get," she responded. I wished her a happy birthday then asked how she succumbed her injuries.

"We had a little thing at home, just us girls but I wanted a stripper this year" she begun.

"Oh Lord', I thought, "another stripper tale. What is happening today?"

"The stripper came over, and by that point we were all mellow from consuming numerous bottles of alcohol. So, I was drunkenly coerced to get on my knees in front of the stripper. We were having clean fun. No touching, no blow job or nothing; he was doing some spinning thing with his penis. So my best friend pulled out her phone to capture the moment. She called out my name and I paused to take the picture but misjudged the distance when I turned to smile for the camera. Next thing I know, his helicopter penis hit me right in my eye during his spin-o-rama. I swear I felt my capillaries rupture. I got a black eye from being whipped by the D." she said laughing uncontrollably once more.

I couldn't help myself either. I chuckled. That story was too funny. Who knew a penis was capable of producing a black eye. This one made my day. I recorded her vitals, updated her docket then sent her to the waiting area. I resumed the paperwork and busied myself until it was time to be relieved for lunch.

****

"Breeeeeeeeeee..." Kim yelled my name from the restaurant's entrance then ran towards me with arms outstretched. We hugged each other tightly and smothered kisses on the cheek. This was our signature for greeting each other.

"I hope you ordered already, because I am starving," I said to her.

"Is there ever a moment when you are not starving", she joked.

I slapped her on the arm for making me seem greedy. We met at one of my favourite spots. The waiters were familiar; every time we visited during lunch hour, we ordered the same thing. I would have a Cobb Salad and Kim would either have a chicken or lobster Alfredo with a glass of Santa Margherita Pinot Grigio. We opted to dine on the outside as usual.

"So what's going on mameee...whats new? How is the Christian life?"

"So far so good. I have been feeling great within and have pretty much been getting things done. Mommy helps me with the scriptures occasionally, and I have been basically taking some time to go through a devotional guide she gave me. This guide makes it a little easier to learn the stories especially since the Bible is somewhat boring to read at times. But I would love to complete it and understand it," she said taking a sip of her water.

"So is there any particular role you are interested to partake in at church? You know like usher, chorister, dancing etc?" I curiously asked.

"Dancing. Me? You know I can't dance to save my life." We both laughed. "But I haven't considered that. I am more focused on reading, understanding the Bible and internalizing God's word."

"Sounds like you have everything planned out. By the way, remember you are hosting the next staging of our girls' night out."

"I know. I was thinking of having it at Wings Fiesta."

"I don't think that is such a good idea. That's your business. You may need to oversee certain things. Besides, who will tend to the customers? You know your mom can't handle that crowd on her own. But I guess if you can find ways to manage all that and still spend quality time with us then by all means."

"I didn't think about that. I guess I may have to take a rain check on hosting this week. Let me sort myself out properly."

"Understood. No rush. Speaking of which…guess who visited me at work today?"

"I don't know. Tell me?" she demanded.

"Alex"

"Alex…. as in Alex, who bought you the car?" Kim asked.

"Yes that same one" I responded.

"What did he want?"

"A lunch or dinner date. He claims there are things I need to know."

"Oh…" The waiter arrived with our meals and refilled our wine glasses.

"So are you going?"

"I don't know. What could he possibly have to say to me that I haven't already heard?" I took up a forkful of the corn with pieces of the avocado and chicken then stuffed my mouth.

"I don't know Bri..Maybe you should hear him out"

"Why am I not surprised by this answer?" I said rolling my eyes.

"It's not like you are dating him all over again. I don't see any harm in giving him a chance to explain himself. And if you go on this lunch or dinner date and you feel sparks kindling, don't be too quick to dismiss it. I know you can be strong willed, but still I think you should just let the emotions flow. You may never know. People change. You just have to give them time. "

"People change yes, but Alex Latouche doesn't change." I scoffed. "He has to be baptized and filled with the Holy Ghost for me to believe that."

She laughed. "He must have really hurt you?"

"You wouldn't even understand" I sighed. "I just don't want to reopen any doors where he is concerned. I know him, and I know that dinner date will be nothing short of him apologizing and making promises he can't keep or him begging me to give him a second chance. I just can't be bothered."

"Well do whatever your gut tells you. Just let me know how it goes." She said taking the final bite of her Alfredo. I don't know how she always managed to eat a whole bowl of that. I was unable to finish a salad much less a plate of noodles.

My lunch hour was coming to an end. We chatted a few more minutes before returning to our regular schedules.

10

Kim

After lunch with Briana, I headed to church to check out the Bible study session they were having for new converts. This was also another opportunity for me to see Duane. I had been crushing on him but was still uncertain as to whether the feeling was mutual, so I played it safe. I must admit that it was difficult for me to stay focused in the session. I felt like I was in high school again. I was never able to sit still and remain focused for more than 30 minutes; after that, I was usually saturated. I wasn't doing too horribly though because I was able to answer a few of the questions at the end of the teaching.

A text message from Bugz came in which read: "I miss you Kim."

I ignored it but then another was received. "I want you."

Those words immediately triggered something inside of me. I yearned for Bugz as well. Truthfully, I yearned for just about any man to be inside of me. I needed the D but I was fighting hard to bury my demons. I turned my phone off so as not to be disturbed any more by his messages. I made an extra effort to cling to every word uttered at that moment through to the end of the

79

class. Duane and I talked for a bit after the session, then I headed home.

I was greeted by Bugz on the outside. I was so surprised. I wasn't even sure how he knew I was here. "You look like you have just seen a ghost?" he said staring at me.

"What are you doing here?"

"I wanted to see you. I miss you. Haven't you seen my messages?"

I ignored his question.

"How did you find me?"

"I have ways and means. Are you going to let me take you home?"

I would love a ride home; but riding with Bugz, I wasn't so sure about.

"I guess that means no. I am sorry to bother you" he said walking away.

For some strange reason, I felt badly about the situation and against better judgement decided to travel with him. My knees were turning into   Jell-O, as I approached the car. I sat in the car and held my bag against my body like a shield. I was charged and horny. I needed to hold it together; that was the only way I would get home without fornicating.

Bugz was not the type to force you to do things you weren't comfortable with, so the ball was in my court. Church and abstinence was a new territory for me so I didn't trust myself around men period. He made casual conversation with me and held my hands as we journeyed home. When we pulled up in my driveway, he unbuckled his seat belt then brushed my hair away from my neck after which he kissed me gently, right above my collarbone. A shiver ran down my spine, and I felt a trickle in my underwear.

"Have a good night Kim."

What the heck?! A part of me wanted to smack him in the face for planting kisses like that on my neck, then left me hanging but then I reminded myself that, that was as far as I was willing to go. I was hesitant to leave the car. I remembered how he kissed my breasts a few days ago and how good they felt in his mouth. I wanted to kiss Bugz hungrily on the lips; but instead, I kissed him on his cheek, thanking him for the ride home then left. I released a long deep sigh of relief the moment I entered my house.

"Lord give me strength; I can tell this journey won't be easy for me."

****

Later that night I received a surprising phone call from Duane. I was hesitant to answer the call, because I certainly didn't want to talk about anything biblical at this hour of the night, especially since I was still hot and bothered from seeing Bugz. I didn't answer his first call, but then when I noticed him calling the third time, I figured it must be urgent. I answered the call slightly annoyed. To my surprise, the call had nothing to do with the church. As a matter of fact, the call was more along the lines of him lusting. I wondered if he was high on something. I couldn't believe the things I was hearing. He expressed how fascinated he was by certain body parts and how much he liked what he saw from the first time I visited the church with my mother. I was elated that attraction was mutual. I had bottled up my feelings for fear of being rejected, so hearing these words were extremely comforting. This meant that there was room for a potential relationship. He suggested meeting tomorrow and I agreed. This would have been our first official date. I had nothing scheduled for tomorrow, so it was great day to hang out.

After ending the telephone conversation, I thought long and hard about ways to improve Wings Fiesta. The business was doing ok, but I wanted more from the venture. I prayed and asked for guidance in making Wings Fiesta a success. I asked the Lord to give me at least one night of good business. I also prayed for protection for Briana and family before ending my prayer, then retired to bed shortly after.

The following morning, I headed out early getting my hair and nails done first. I wanted to look my best for Duane. After that, I rushed to a few boutiques in an attempt to find a cute outfit. I was searching intensely through one of the clothing racks, when I noticed a gentle man watching me closely from the other side of the room. Usually, fixed stares made me paranoid but I was so desperate to find an outfit that I was unbothered by him. So much so, that I failed to realize that he ended up in the same aisle with me. I glanced in his direction for a few seconds, then proceeded to ponder between the two dresses I had in my hand.

"I think the one with the V-cut would look amazing on you." I heard him say.

"What do you know about women's fashion," I shot back feistily.

" I may not be a fashionista, but what I am absolutely sure about is that a woman with such curvature and bust would rock the hell out of that   v-cut, and if you opt for a brighter colour like red in that design, that would only seal the deal" he quipped.

I scrutinized the dress once more, this time taking his advice into consideration. Maybe he was right. I would look gorgeous in this.

"Thank you," I finally said.

"You are most welcome. Big date later?"

"You think because you recommended an outfit means you are privy to know my whereabouts?" I was a little annoyed.

"I am sorry. That was rude of me. I am Hugh Brenton, by the way," he said with arms extended for a hand shake.

"I am Kimberly." I shook his hand.

"Nice to meet you Kim. Would you be able to spare me a few minutes of your time to have drinks with me."

"Are you always this forward with women you meet?"

"Yes. I am asking you to lunch or drinks. It's either a yes or a no. I don't see what's there to think about."

Who does this man think he is; he was so blunt, but I kind of liked it.

"Well in the event you changed your mind, here is my card. I am staying at a hotel a few blocks from here so, you are welcome to stop by if you reconsider." He flashed me a smile that made my knees buckle. He collected his package from the cashier then left.

"I think you should go with the v-cut," said one of the ladies who was working the floor.

"Yes. I think I will definitely get this one," I said smiling.

"You know you should have drinks with him. He is rich, and I hear he spoils his women."

I looked at her slightly confused.

"Mr Brenton, the man who just gave you his card."

It seems like being nosey was the criteria for being in this store.

"Ok thanks." I said before making my way to the cashier. I pulled out my phone and googled him quickly. He was the CEO of a well-known company; that meant he was financially stable. Maybe I should reconsider and have drinks for a few minutes with him. I called the number but there was no answer, so I made a bold move and showed up to the hotel instead.

"Hi Good Afternoon, I am here to see Mr. Hugh Brenton", I said to the woman at the front desk who eye balled me from head to toe before acknowledging me.

"What's your name?"

"Tell him Kimberly..." I responded. I waited and watched as she dialed his room.

"He will be down shortly. You may have a seat if you wish."

"Thank you." I paced the floor and looked around the lobby with adrenaline flooding my veins as I awaited Mr Brenton's arrival.

I shot a glance over my shoulder at the sound of an elevator door opening, only to see Hugh Brenton heading towards the lobby, with his thumb hooked in the belt loop of his jeans, flashing his gorgeous smile, first at me then at the woman at the front desk.

I approached him and waited as he spoke with the woman about extending his stay. She looked like she was unbuttoning his shirt with her eyes, as she listened to his requests. Very unprofessional, I thought. Then again, I supposed a man of his caliber was a magnet for women. I slipped my arms around Hugh's waist and beckoned for him to leave because by now that woman had taken off his shirt and was licking his chest.

I am not even sure why I felt jealous about a man I didn't know, but I did. I pulled Hugh away because that woman was getting on my nerves.

The hotel room was a gleaming, beige coloured box of understated luxury. A bottle of champagne waited in a silver wine bucket and there were gourmet chocolates arranged on the pillows. I stood in the centre of the beautiful room and my old life flashed before me. Suddenly, I was a little scared. I was scared because, I needed to bury my demons and it seems like I kept walking down the path of temptations. I snatched one of the chocolates and ate it nervously. If I didn't turn tail and run right now, I was afraid I may do something I would regret later. He poured me a glass and we talked for a little while. Though he seemed arrogant when I met him earlier, he was way nicer and calmer now.

"Am I allowed to ask you to fit that dress for me that you purchased earlier? I hope you bought the V-Cut."

"Yes I did." I gladly tried it on as I was curious to see how it would fit as well. I was impressed. I actually loved the way it accentuated my curves. Hugh marveled about the way I looked, and I couldn't help myself from blushing. That's when it dawned on me that if I didn't leave soon, I was bound to be late for my date with Duane. I looked at my watch as I tried to figure out the best way to pace my activities.

"What time is your date?"

"You don't give up, do you?"

"Well I mean, you keep glancing at your watch which is an indicator that there is somewhere you need to be. I feel privileged that you squeezed me in, but I wouldn't want you to be late."

"It is in three hours."

"Do you think you will be able to make it home in time to freshen up and still be on time?" He looked at me as if trying to entice me to stay.

"I doubt it. I will call him to push back the time."

"Or I could take you there. You could get dressed from here and I drop you off. I can leave you at a distance from your meeting spot, if you don't want him to see another man dropping you off."

"But I wouldn't have any accessories or shoes to go with the dress if I left from here."

Without hesitation he said, "We could go back to the mall and get you something."

"You would go back to the mall to purchase accessories to complete an outfit for a woman going out on a date with another man plus allow her to get dressed in your presence and drop her off" I said, carefully reiterating the details in an effort to point out the absurdity of his suggestion.

"Yes…because I see something I like and I don't give up easily on things I desire. I will go the extra mile, so in the event the little date doesn't work out, you will consider me plan b."

We both laughed in unison.

"And even though I think you will look just as gorgeous without accessories, if that's what you really want then we can get it," he stated, stepping even closer to me. Next thing I knew, his lips moved up my neck, his tongue touching my skin ever so lightly. He traced a finger along my jawline and then slowly drew it down again, stopping at the v-cut of the dress. I waited, trembling for him to slip his hands inside and grab my boobs, but he didn't.

"So what's it going to be?" he asked.

Lord forgive me because I am about to sin. One last time Lord, then I promise I am done; no more sex.

"Make love to me," I said breathily. He reached around my back and found the slender zipper. He gave a sharp tug and the dress slid down my body. I stood there exposed, breathless and horny as ever. He grabbed me and we kissed deeply. He then reached under me, lifted me up and I wrapped my legs around his waist as he walked towards the bed and laid me down on it. He placed his mouth on my breasts and I gasped.

Oh yes...I am really doing this. Gosh this feels so good.

His tongue went all over my body. He paused a minute then undressed. I wriggled out of my underwear while he did that. I stretched out my arms and pulled him onto me. When he thrust himself inside me, I cried out, rocking against his hips, kissing his shoulders and piercing my fingers in his back. I pulled him into me with all my strength as the heat inside me rose in waves. When I cried out in release, my nails dug even deeper into his back. A moment later he cried out too and then he collapsed on top of me panting. I don't usually get to my destination so quickly, but I guess it had really been awhile.

"Oh God you are awesome," I said looking to the heavens, as my body experienced occasional tremors as I tried to recover from the orgasm just now. Spent, we both slept for a little while. Thanks to Hugh, I was awakened with just enough time to go back to mall to purchase footwear and accessories as planned. I ate and got dressed from his room; after which, he dropped me off at the theatre.

"Kimberly, that was an incredible lunch date, could I interest you in a dinner date soon?" He appeared smitten, yet confident.

I smiled back at him. "Sure. Thanks again." I said before kissing him good bye.

****

As soon as I entered the theatre, it was all smiles. I was on a high from my encounter with Hugh. For a brief moment, I wondered if I would be able to date them both if I had difficulties choosing one. I was still attracted to Duane but now I also had interest in Hugh. Duane smiled from ear to ear the moment our eyes met. He hugged me and greeted me with warm kisses on the cheek. We made our way to the food station and bought a jumbo popcorn to be shared between us. He placed his hands around my waist as we headed towards the cinema. This is something I could easily get used to.

90

It was nice to see another side to him. No suit, no tie, no pocket square, just simple jeans and Tee's with a very relaxing vibe to it. I felt proud to be his date and strutted my sexiness confidently beside him. I appreciated the way he related to me, as if I was his woman. We talked for a little while but as soon as the movie begun, the conversation ended abruptly. Neither of us wanted to miss a second of the movie. Though we weren't conversing, he held my hands throughout the movie. However, what took me by surprise was his bold move to kiss me in the theatre. I was hesitant at first but couldn't help but return the gesture after feeling how soft and moist his lips were. He was clearly oblivious to the persons seated next to us as his kisses deepened and his tongue traversed the crevices of my mouth. When he eventually released me for air, I remained still with my eyes closed. Duane's kisses were followed by flash backs of my lunch date with Hugh.

My emotions were all over the place where both men were concerned. I eased myself down in the seat then stared at Duane for a moment before smiling back at him. All I saw, was how adorable he seemed to be. I wasn't sure how this would play out, but I knew I needed him in my life, and I would also like to keep Hugh close. I ran my hands along his legs then held his hands as soon as the movie resumed. By this time, I was satiated from almost half of the jumbo bucket of popcorn. The truth is, I was still somewhat full from the food I had during my earlier escapade with Hugh, but tried my best to have a little of what Duane purchased, in order for it not to seem like a waste of his money. He ended up finishing the other half on his own. We remained seated hand in hand until the movie ended.

We headed to the car and sat inside for another hour, talking about any and every thing that came to mind. We exchanged passionate kisses once more, but this moment was interrupted by a security guard knocking on our window. Apparently, he was informing us about the closure of the premises, so we had to leave. We were so engrossed in the conversation that we failed to realize that we were basically the only ones left in the parking lot. Speaking of which, Duane also earned points in my good book, because he owned a vehicle.

When all was said and done, I had a great day. Two dates in one day which both turned out amazing. I was a happy camper. I kissed him good night and he made sure I went inside the house safely before driving off.

"God you are awesome. Thank you for making me have such an amazing day."

My cell phone vibrated and Duane's name came up on the caller id.

"Miss me already?" I cooed into the headset.

"Most definitely, but that's not the reason I called."

"Oh...what is the reason then?"

"I didn't get a chance to tell you how gorgeous you looked tonight. You wore that dress very well; it was breath-taking actually."

I soaked up the compliment and for some strange reason, I could barely manage to say thanks, that's how much I was blushing.

"Anyway, I won't keep you up any longer. Thanks for going out with me tonight. I really enjoyed your company. I want you to be part of my life, provided that the feeling is mutual of course?"

I took this to mean that he was indirectly asking me to be his woman.

"Yes..I would love that," I responded.

"Great. Well alrighty then. We will talk tomorrow. Sweet dreams baby girl. Good night."

"Good Night D.."

With that, I kicked off my slipper then flung myself onto the bed. I reminisced once more on my day.

"Thank you Lord. You are great indeed," I said once more before drifting to sleep.

11

Briana

By the time I walked to my car in the parking lot at 7pm, I had had a full day. I stopped at the red Honda station wagon I drove, unlocked it, and threw my hand bag, /lunch bags and other luggage's on the back seat. I pinned up my hair, flung my head back on the seat and breathed a long sigh of relief that my shift was over. I couldn't help but to mentally replay my day as I journeyed home. I yearned to get home to my warm cup of coffee and my swinging chair. As I made the turn to pull up in my driveway, my peace of mind was disturbed by the mere sight of Chris parked there. I hadn't spoken to him since I had seen him in the supermarket with a woman and two kids looking like the perfect family.

I was totally flabbergasted to see him traversing the supermarket aisles with hands neatly placed on the small of her back and the kids yelling daddy. I was so angry that day. He lied to me. Memories of my exe'-s immediately tormented me. I couldn't believe I fell for the wrong person for a third time. Boy I sure knew how to pick them. I shook my head in disbelief. I was completely blindsided by this one. I was so shocked that I almost denied the evidence that was standing right in front of me. This man slept at my house on numerous occasions, we engaged in activities after work, sometimes we car pooled and not to mention our many weekend getaways. I swore I commanded his attention and the harder I tried to put things into perspective, the more confused I became. I couldn't understand where or how there was room for a wife. Where had she been all this time we were frolicking. I needed him to know that I saw him. I turned my head away and pushed the trolley in his direction bumping into the wife and her trolley. I apologized profusely for "accidentally" bumping into her while simultaneously watching Chris through the corners of my eyes. After she reassured me that she was ok, I made sure Chris and I saw eye to eye before I moved off. I hadn't said a word to him since and he made no effort to contact me either, until, this very moment, being present in my driveway.

"Go home to your skinny ass wife"; the words snapped out of my mouth as I strolled pass him with my baggage's.

He gave me a look like he would beat my ass if he thought he could get away with it.

"Don't talk about my wife."

His words of protection for the woman he chose over me, drove me over the edge. I spun around immediately and slapped him with my bags; then before I could stop myself, my hand left my side and slapped him across the face. The red mark swelled on his skin. The silence that followed scared me to death. In that instant, he reached up and whacked me on my cheek.

The sound and force of his hand made me gasp in shock. A man had never laid his hands on me. The fury intensified. I dropped all bags to the floor and landed a few punches to his chest. He caught my arms in his on the fourth punch and gripped them firmly. I was helpless at this point. He waited for me to calm down before releasing me. I picked up my bags from the floor and proceeded to open the front door. I entered the house and Chris followed behind. I remained silent while I unpacked my bags. I then proceeded to make my coffee. I needed it well strong in order for it to counteract all the emotions that was stirred by Chris. While making coffee, the devil on my shoulder encouraged me to burn Chris with it but fortunately for him, I didn't listen.

"Honey, can you please talk to me." He said apologetically.

"Get out my house?" I yelled back.

"You have all right to be angry, but can we please talk?"

"There is nothing to talk about Chris. We have been living a lie. I don't see what we need to discuss." He attempted to hold me but I dodged him. He made a second attempt but I moved once more. "Don't touch me", I screamed and threatened him with the hot cup of coffee laying on the counter.

"You wouldn't dare"

"Try me," I said looking dead in his eyes. I took a sip of my coffee which immediately had a soothing effect.

"Briana, I need you"

"You have a wife, you don't need anything more."

"Yes, I do but you and I have something special and...."

I interrupted his sentence. I took another long sip of my coffee before continuing. "You and I have nothing special. You are selfish for doing this to me. You know that nothing long term can result from this relationship, and yet you used me. You are selfish for doing this. You didn't even give me a choice? Did you ever plan on telling me, you were married?"

"I didn't think it mattered Bri.."

"Why wouldn't it matter? You would have prevented me from wasting my precious time with you."

"You didn't waste your time sweety. We can still create many more memories and maybe even start a family."

"You are married. How are we going to have a family; don't even bullshit me with the I am planning to leave my wife line; I swear I will empty this cup of coffee in your face."

"We don't have to be married to have children sweety…"

"Umm having a child with another woman's husband; at least, I should say, knowingly planning to conceive in a situation like this is not something I am cool with. I can't believe you would even think like that. It really shows that you don't care about me. I should forever be your side piece." I looked at him in disbelief. "I really can't believe you would say that," only this time my voice cracked and I fought back the tears. I placed the cup on the counter and wiped the few tear drops that managed to escape.

Chris approached and grabbed me, placing my arms behind me onto the kitchen wall and held me captive. I squirmed to get free.

"Get off me! " I yelled, wriggling in his grip. I didn't come close to matching Chris' strength, but I fought anyway. Fighting only pressed me closer to him and the closer I got the more my vagina tingled. The wriggling to free myself and him deliberately exerting his body against mine made my vagina dripped. I am sure he sensed it. I hated this man for the effect he had on me. I stopped squirming and focused my stare on the floor.

"Look at me," his voice came out as a bark, but I ignored him. He bent closer whispering into my ear. "I am sorry. I have never hit a woman in my life. I am really sorry Briana. If you don't want to believe anything I have said to you; believe that."

Those words forced me to face him.

"Right... lying to women is more your speed." I hissed.

"Look at me," and this time I did. His body pressed even closer, sucking all the air out from between us.

"You...you need to leave", I stuttered, confusion giving me away.

"Is that what you really want?" his voice got all throaty and sexy.

What the heck was happening with me? One week without sex could not have driven me to lose my good sense. *Briana snap out of it....Get it together.. You don't need Chris. The man is married Briana. Leave people's husband alone.* I warned myself, but my body insisted on betraying me.

"Go home Chris." I said breathily in his ear.

"Is that your final answer?" he questioned, his voice dropping down into a sexier octave.

"Yes." I tried my best to sound convincing. He challenged me.

"No, it isn't sweety"

"Yes, it is my final answer. Please go"

"If that's what you really want, then I will go." He pushed his pelvis close to my groin, and before I could stop it, a murmur of pleasure escaped from my mouth.

"Go home to your wife Chris."

"I don't want to go home to her. I want to be with you." As proof, he pressed his rock hard penis against my thigh.

"Stop," I tried to fight him but the combination of his hot breath on my neck and the familiarity of his hard penis rendered me powerless. It felt like this man had whipped some kryptonite on my ass.

One more time wouldn't be the end of the world; I tried to reason with myself.

"Tell me you want me to stay and make love to you", he demanded.

"No," I whined.

"Say it,'' he said firmly

Everything in me melted. I wanted this man so badly, and he knew it.

"Please leave...." My voice failed.

His lips lightly touched the tip of my ear. An electric current shot through my body, releasing any residual fantasy that I could walk away or force him to leave.

My vagina sent smoke signals to his penis and there was no way he would release me from his grip.

"I want you to stay."

"Stay and do what?" he asked.

"Make love to me," I begged, feeling the juice trickle down my legs. How could I be so cruel to myself? I needed satisfaction. Just one more night; one more for the road. I wouldn't allow myself to think about the consequences. I only know that in this moment, everything I wanted or needed was right here pressed against me. I melted into his arms and gave myself to him completely.

****

I woke him up in the wee hours of the morning and sent him home once more. I couldn't believe he was married. How could I have seen the signs? It bothered me so much, I couldn't return to sleep. I messaged Kim and told her what had happened. She immediately dismissed it because he was married. Church really had a way of changing people because the Kim back then would have taken the bait, married or not. I eventually ended the conversation, didn't want to keep her up any longer but I think primarily because she wasn't exactly telling me what I wanted to hear. I was still in turmoil because I didn't want to let go off Chris. The sex was too good. I had finally found a nice replacement for Alex, only to find out that he is married. Sometimes I wondered if someone placed some form of curse on my love life. It cannot be normal for someone to back to back have horrible relationships. A text message came in from Chris telling me that he was safely home interrupted my thoughts. Then a few seconds later, another one received which read "I *miss you already*." I didn't respond to that message; I didn't want to.

My thoughts drifted again. I tried to remember all the encounters we have had, and I slowed them down and tried to pin point anything that would have suggested he was married; still, there was nothing. The only one fact that I always found odd, was that he was rarely on his phone. Whenever we were together, there was never a phone call or text message or anything to disturb us. I just thought that meant he was just all about me and simply wanted to give me his undivided attention. How could I have been so stupid? I tried to avoid Chris since our last interaction, but my attempts have been unsuccessful.

Since our fight and subsequent make up session that night, I vowed to myself that would have been the last round with Chris and promised that I would trod the celibacy path. Unfortunately for me, that one round lead to many more rounds which in turn lead to many more days, nights and weekends spent together, but we had a mutual understanding. It was just sex; nothing more. We no longer did dinner dates or any adventurous outings; it was just plain, raunchy, unadulterated sex. I was his booty call, and I was ok with this title for the time being. I assumed the role of that woman in his life who would grant all his fantasies and quenched his cravings. We had a mutually healthy sexual relationship. I never asked details about his wife because I had the notion that the less I knew, the more willing and more relaxed I would have been in the agreement. That way, it was harder for me to become emotionally attached to Chris or have a change of heart because I somehow felt sympathetic towards his wife. I knew for sure that he loved her and would never leave her. Though he never mentioned it, I just knew it.

I was comfortable with our relationship, so much so that I suggested granting him a ménage a trois for his birthday which was in a few weeks. So shocked by my proposal, he hesitated before telling me that my idea was too much for him. I insisted because I knew that it was most men's dream to have sex with multiple women at once. It had always been a fantasy of his, so I wasn't sure why he was so hesitant. In order to get him to take the bait, I told him that he was in full control as it relates to choosing the third person, but under one condition, that she had a nice ass and a reasonable size breast. He was still hesitant and pensive. I couldn't understand why. When I eventually asked what he feared why he was hesitant. He mentioned that he feared someone becoming emotionally attached. I highlighted the fact that we had been doing this agreement for quite a while with his wife at play and I hadn't been emotionally attached to date so it was highly unlikely that would happen now. I told him that factor would more likely apply to the third candidate. His second concern was what would happen if he was not able to satisfy us both or maybe became too excited about having two women at once that he finished the job too quickly. I laughed at the thought of this. In my rush to offer him a once in a lifetime sexual experience, I didn't think about any of this. My only concern was the thrill of the act and nothing else. I told him that if he had that many concerns that we could scrap the idea. The truth is, there would be no fun in him participating in something he wasn't comfortable with. But then he still insisted and asked for more details. After hours of deliberation, he eventually agreed. I was so excited and immediately couldn't wait for the day to come. Admittedly, I was more excited about the ménage a trois than the actual birthday.

12

KIM

Duane was my new boyfriend. Although, he didn't officially ask the question and neither of us made any attempts to officially discuss it, we related to each other as if we were. We spent quality time together and spoke on the phone on days we were not together. He has stayed at my house a few times for dinner, and mommy loved him. The fact that he worships the Lord, earned him a few points in her good book. Duane and I were happy. There were moments when I wished the devil tempted him as often as he did me, because he had never uttered suggestive remarks nor did he ever acted inappropriately towards me. Despite this, we were good together....we were cool.

****

Wings Fiesta was frustrating me, as the last few Fridays had been terribly slow, I was unable to breakeven. Things went from bad to worse last Friday, that I was unable to pay my workers but I managed to gather money from other sources. Not having money at my disposal and in abundance was working my nerves. Business this month was terrible. I was unable to provide my portion to the utility bills. I barely earned sufficient funds to put food on the table this month. Thankfully, I had a mother who always found ways to make ends meet, no matter what. She covered most of the expenses, and I was grateful.

God had blessed me with a good man but he hadn't gotten around to blessing my career and my finances. This type of hardship made me realize that I needed to rely more on God, so I decided to participate in the one week of prayer and fasting activity that was happening at church. I needed financial freedom, and I was willing to start fasting for it.

After completing my usual lunch duties at the school, I headed over to church for one of the usual prayer services held on that day. But something unusual happened to me. In the midst of prayer, I had the spirit of guilt and shame placed upon me. I felt badly about how dishonest I had been with myself and my way of life that was not entirely in accordance with what I preached. I had flashbacks about my sinful encounter with Hugh, and I felt awful. I cried uncontrollably at the altar and asked the Lord for forgiveness. I prayed for strength and endurance on my quest to serve the Lord whole-heartedly.

I sat quietly throughout the rest of the meeting, because I felt ashamed about the things I had done. I listened keenly to the word and I was reminded about how steadfast I needed to be when life seemed to be testing me. Tests in life were not only based on the last lesson learned but instead on the application of prior lessons. I was reminded of how important it was to stay focused on the objective during any test, even when it seemed extremely difficult. I reminded myself that sometimes when we are going through a hard time, it may seem like our situation is set out to highlight our inadequacies or frustrate and challenge us but that it may be God's way of taking us to another level. We must be able to hold tight and push through the obstacles to achieve greatness.

I made up my mind that evening to try harder in standing firm in the word of God. Duane and I headed for ice cream after church; he then took me home.

13

Briana

I jammed my hand hard against the horn. "Why is everyone driving so slowly?" I yelled. I hit the steering wheel once more. "Oh my gossssh, can you move!!!" I screamed before gripping the wheel even tighter and screamed even louder. "Would everyone just get off the damn road?" I shouted at the cars in front of me. If I wanted to be honest with myself, I would admit that my horrible mood had nothing to do with the traffic I was in. But it was so much easier to use this as an excuse than to face the truth. I gripped the wheel once more as I tried to hold back my frustration and the tears that were ready to burst forth. I really thought I had this all planned out; I didn't see this coming at all. I really messed up. But I had no one to blame but myself. All I wanted was to make him happy. But then it seemed like I made him a little bit too happy and now I hated his guts and everyone around me. Tears streamed down my face as memories of the event pervaded my thoughts with vengeance. My mind was like a DVD player on continuous loop. Chris caressing her body with his tongue, blowing kisses along her thighs, hoisting her legs on his shoulders then penetrated her slowly and gently as if trying to hit a nerve in her body. The same movements he had done to me thousands of times in the past.

"You like that baby? Do you like how I feel inside you?" he asked pushing himself even deeper inside her. "Oh God..Yes.Yes..Yeeeees..." was all she screamed. I closed my eyes and opened them again, praying that it would be enough to earn a few seconds of peace from the nightmare that was playing out in front of me. He totally ignored me. I felt like last year's hot Christmas toy, tossed aside by a child who had gotten something new and more exciting to play with.

"Yes Chris...don't stop. That feels so good. You are so big. Yes....Yes...right there." She moaned. She was so full of shit. I don't know why the hell she was hollering and carrying on as if she was being touched for the very first time. Watching him thrust deeper inside her coupled with her screams piercing my ear drums made my stomach queasy.

He had this look of intense concentration and pleasure that made me want to strangle him. Homeboy was clearly having way too much fun. He handled her with such care, such intimacy; he handled her like he would handle me. I wanted to smack the shit out of him for being such a gentleman to this alien in our bedroom. This Alien he was probably having an affair with now that I am thinking about it. How did he manage to find someone so quickly? There must have been some form of courting prior to this. Maybe they even had sexual encounters; after all he was cheating on his wife with me. What would make it any different for it not to happen to me? My thoughts were interrupted by a bus driver who basically attempted to "undertake" the line of traffic almost brushing against my vehicle. I put the windows down shooting him an evil glare. This was obviously unintentional but seemed to be my natural expression at the moment.

"Easy nuh boss lady," he said as he did a hand signal indicating that he didn't touch my vehicle. "It's all good," he said as he honked his horn once more before driving off to rejoin the line of traffic. I put some music on to help settle my emotions, but it wasn't long before the birthday nightmare resurfaced.

So after almost being strangled by jealousy of this woman taking over my man, I decided to intervene. She had gotten more than enough of my Chris. There was nothing satisfying about this scene. Watching another woman squirm with pleasure beneath my man was absolutely horrid to watch. It was disgusting really but I already consented to this horror movie, so might as well try to enjoy the show. I stroked his arms then worked my way towards his back where I ran my fingers along his spine, then he finally glanced at me but with a painstaking expression of ecstasy across his face that told me I was messing up his concentration and I just needed to wait my turn. Chris wanted me to wait my turn to get his D...

This cant be happening! If I had a gun, I swear there would have been a murder suicide. A few minutes later he had the nerve to look back in my direction uttering the words "I love you baby...I love this; this is the best gift," while never ceasing to dip deeper and deeper between her thighs. A few minutes later, she hollered she was about to come. I guess now it would have been my turn. Reality setback in and the images faded. I was back in my car again. The soul music that came on made me mad, so I switched to dancehall; something more upbeat. I tried to rock and create a little vibe while moving in the slow crawl of afternoon traffic. I picked up my phone and scrolled through my messages, skipping over all received from Chris. I wasn't sure how to approach the situation. It's been two days since the encounter, but it was eating me alive, meanwhile I am sure he still was on cloud nine basking in happiness. We never spoke of the ordeal but I wanted badly to bring it up without starting a fight. I don't even know why I was flipping out and he didn't even belong to me. That was one of the reasons I decided to do such a thing with Chris. I really didn't think I cared about him that much. I had never before- been jealous of him, so I was not sure what it was about this woman that made me crazy. This was supposed to have been a walk in the park encounter; like nothing happened. I needed to get my shit together before arriving at the children's home. I certainly didn't want to be in a foul mood in their presence. It had been a while since I last visited due to my hectic work schedule, and I wasn't about to miss out this time because I was having difficulty sorting through my personal issues. After all, the organization only visited this children's home twice monthly, so they needed my undivided attention.

I thought about calling Kim and reached for my cell but like magic, the phone rang and her name showed up on the caller id.

YES...saved by the bestie. I thought.

"Hey girl...Whats up?"

"Bri..I can't do this. I don't think I can do this."

"Can't do what?"

"I need to start hustling again. I need nice things. I am not liking being ordinary and living ordinary. The cooking gig has been slow recently, so I am not making much and when I do, all I do is break even. I need to have a steady influx of cash at all times." She sighed.

"Kim, you need to calm down. Remember all this come with the territory of operating a business. This minute you may have customers and a nice influx whereas a next moment you may have little or none. You can't give up when you have slow days. You can't give up the moment you stumble upon an obstacle. Sometimes God creates these setbacks because He wants to teach us a lesson. Sometimes He is preparing you for what is to come but some of us need to learn certain things first before we can be introduced to the ultimate place He wants us to be; so he holds you back.

You need to trust him and believe that he will work things out in your favour, no matter what."

"It's so amazing that you are telling me the same thing they spoke to us about in prayer meeting the other day, but it's so hard. I have been praying about the situation. I have been praying that He opens another door for me if He sees this one is not working out but..."

I interrupted her.

"That is what I am saying Kim. You need to be patient. Notice you said, you prayed for another opportunity window **if** He thinks it's not working out. You can't say the business is not working out because you have had slow days. You are too hasty to give up. I am no saint, but one thing I can personally attest to, is that He is an on time God. He may not come when you want Him but He will be there when He thinks the time is right. I can't emphasize this anymore. You just need to trust him. Prayer without faith is useless. You need to believe that He is more than able to grant your desires and bless you abundantly."

"I swear I don't know why you are like that. You always have things under control. I feel like your level of faith in a God you don't even worship has exceeded mine, no offense."

"None taken," I said laughing. "I know what you mean."

"You need to revisit my church Bri.."

"Maybe I do, but I wouldn't count on it." I said.

"As you said, prayer moves mountains, so I will pray about it," she said.

"No don't pray that prayer." I responded. We both burst out in laughter.

"FINALLY!" I said after realizing the road was suddenly clear after passing the intersection.

"What..What happen?" asked Kim.

"I have been stuck in traffic all morning and now the road is finally clear. I am heading to a children's home with my charity group. Remember I usually visit at least once monthly with them?"

" Oh yes.. yes..I remember. Maybe we can have drinks or something later?"

"I am not sure yet. I think I may be out with Chris."

"Oh, he is still in the picture, how has he been?'

"That's another story," I said as the images floated in my thoughts.

"We will catch up. Love you. Have a great day" I said before ending the call. I pulled up in the parking lot of the home and remained in the car for a few more minutes. I needed Jesus to sort through my messy social life. Maybe I should apply my own advice and pray. I took deep breaths then released long deep sighs in an attempt to amp myself up for my eventful day. I whispered a short prayer before setting off to see the kids.

****

I quickly settled in, unpacked and tried to sort through the boxes of toys and clothing that persons had donated. I had separated the clothing based on age and gender prior to arriving, so my work load was not as much but then a light brush against my leg threw me off balance almost making me scream, only to realize it was only Joshua. Joshua was the most adorable 4 year old I had ever met. He was not only handsome but so full of character. I often wondered how such a sweetheart like him ended up in a home. How could a parent not want to keep such bundle of joy? Sometimes being around some of these children made me emotional when I think about the cruelty some of them had endured. I thought it was so unfair to them to be tossed aside by people who were supposed to love and nurture them. They were so innocent. My heart ached at times when I interacted with them but being a part of this charity organization made me realize how privileged I was so, I became more appreciative and content with what I have.

Joshua became attached to me, and I to him, from my first visit to the home. There was something about him that resonated with me. I told myself that if and when I became more financially stable, I would definitely adopt him if he wasn't placed with a family. Joshua made me extremely happy and he was certainly my favourite, but I tried to give every child my undivided attention so as to minimize the possibilities of jealousy among the kids. I picked him up then smothered his cheeks with kisses, and he loved this.

While playing with Joshua, my eye caught an unfamiliar face. He was looking casually smart sporting a white dress shirt with French cuffs, slim fit cotton blend chinos with a pair of dark brown brogues. He was nicely attired for a white man. His demeanor screamed power and authority. I watched him keenly as he strut his sexiness from one room to the next. I wondered if he was a new recruit, but then he seemed like too much of a CEO or something along those lines to be a part of an organization like this. People like him were more responsible for writing cheques and working behind the scenes rather than carrying out an actual visit. The sound of a dry, persistent cough from Joshua interrupted my moment of lust.

Joshua became a bit irritable, so I pampered him in order to calm him down. It wasn't long before he asked for juice, so I placed him on the floor and gave him a few toys to play with while I fetched his drink. I bumped into another member of the organization that I hadn't seen in a while, so we chatted for a few minutes before I returned to Joshua. To my surprise, he was being tossed in the air occasionally by Mr. Well-dressed. By the sound of Joshua's high pitched laughter, there was no doubt he was enjoying himself. This was a nice moment.

"Careful, wouldn't want him to soil your white shirt?"

"I can always wash it," he responded.

"Ok then. Now that is a line I don't hear often" I thought.

"What...You don't think I am capable of doing my own laundry?" he asked

I laughed. "No..no...I wasn't thinking that;" I stuttered.

"Are you sure because that is not what the look on your face is telling me.?"

I could never do a good job masking my thoughts; my face always revealed what I was thinking.

"You look too dapper to be playing with kids; dirty kids too." I said in defense. He laughed and this made him look even more handsome. The dimple sealed the deal. He was a ten in my eyes.

"Hi, I am Steve," he said extending his arms in my direction with the other carefully holding Joshua.

"I am Briana," I said extending warmth and friendliness. He had a firm grip.

"Are you here with a group?" I asked.

"No I am not. The home has requested financial assistance from my organization, so I decided to deliver the cheque personally because I was going to be in the vicinity.

I knew it, I thought. Joshua reached for the drink in my hand that I had totally forgotten about.

"You must really like this one..." he said. I looked at him confused. "Your whole mannerism in dealing with him, tells me that you either love children or you are just really fascinated by this one? What's his name?"

"Joshua" I responded.

"So are you in love with Joshua or do you just love children?"

"I am in love with Joshua," I responded.

"Do you have any children of your own?" he asked.

"No I don't, but sometimes I feel like I would make Joshua my own."

"So why don't you?"

"I am just not ready."

"You are not ready or you don't think your boyfriend will accept that?"

"Are you always this forward?" I asked.

"No. I am sorry. I really didn't mean to offend you in anyway. I guess what I really want to ask is for your number but I wasn't sure how to. After all, I didn't come over here because I thought Joshua was handsome."

We both laughed. "So, you have been watching me?" I asked with a flirtatious smirk.

"Just like you have been eyeballing me" he shot back. "So since we know for sure that we both like what we see, how about we get to know each other?" he asked once more, only this time more subtly.

I paused for a moment. He was handsome and looked like he knew what he was about. Furthermore, I guess it wouldn't hurt to date someone from another race. I was beyond frustrated with the men I have dated. I even contemplated dating a woman; black men were stressing me out. I asked for his phone and entered my name and number.

"Will you even remember me?" I asked to reassure myself that I wasn't wasting my time.

"You can save it as the girl from the children's home," he responded.

My face went from all smiles to stone cold.

"I am just teasing," he quickly added. "I will call you Briana," he said as he took the phone from my hand. He remembered my name; that was a good sign. "Now that my mission is accomplished, I can head back to work now," he said handing Joshua over to me. I couldn't contain the laughter. I shook my head as I watched him walk away.

A group of boys approached Joshua, and they all ran off to play. I resumed my task of unpacking; after which, I assisted the other members in bathing and grooming a few of the kids. I had Steve in my thoughts the whole time. I was excited about getting to know him. A few minutes later a text came in from an unknown number which read "BTW, you have a very lovely ass."

I smiled and proceeded with my duties, occasionally checking my messages. This was pretty much my routine for the rest of the day. Between taking care of the kids, texting Steve and of course loving up my Joshua, my day ended on a good note in contrast to the awful morning I had.

****

Telephone conversations between Chris and I had not really been a thing since the ménage a trois, but tonight was one of the nights he would usually come by after work. I planned to discuss the matter with him before it drove me to the nuthouse because the moment I entered my house, the images resurfaced. I turned on the TV and let the news headlines distract me. For a few minutes, I succeeded. I tried to retract my steps and penciled out my thoughts. Why was I so worked up about another woman's husband? I led myself to believe that because I had no obligation to this man that I could comfortably do whatever I wanted and not feel guilty. With this thought in mind, I was convinced he was the perfect candidate to fulfill a fantasy I always desired. No emotional attraction; no strings attached. But what I failed to foresee was the post menage a trois repercussions. I never thought about the possibilities of him enjoying her more than me, and it was eating me alive. They were so into each other, they might have been happier if I hadn't been in the room at all. Then their asses could have screwed each other all night long. How could I not have seen this?

The sound of a vehicle being armed signaled Chris's arrival; this drew me back to reality. I tried hard to control my inner bitch waiting to come out. Starting a fight with him the minute he came through the door was not the best way to approach this problem. I tried to act as normal as possible, so I mustered the most pleasant look, as I opened the door to let him in.

He greeted me with a warm kiss on my cheeks then lips before stepping past me and headed towards the kitchen. He picked up a bottle of Zinfandel and fixed us both a glass. "So how was your day?" he asked as he turned to look at me.

"It was ok. I spent the day at a children's home with my charity group. You know it's always a pleasure being around those kids. "What about yours?" I asked.

"Pretty uneventful," he shrugged before heading towards the bathroom.

I promised myself I wasn't going to let my jealousy rear its ugly head, but this bullshit small talk just wasn't cutting it for me. "Honey can I ask you a question?"

He hesitated before giving a response. "Go ahead dear. What's on your mind?"

"Did you enjoy the other night."

"I enjoyed every moment of it. You are the best girlfriend ever." He washed his hands then approached me and kissed me on the lips sporting a wide grin.

"Would you do it again?"

"Of course!!" he responded. I am sure Tasha would love that too.

"Why would you do it with Tasha again though?" I asked.

"What do you mean? She enjoyed it...I enjoyed it...You enjoyed it. We all had chemistry, so why not? No need to complicate things with new people.

"We all had chemistry?" I scuffed icily.

Those words wiped the grin off his face. He now had a raised eyebrow. "What is that supposed to mean?" A brief look of panic crossed his face. There was no sense in side-stepping the issue now, so I got right to the point.

"Did you have sexual relations with Tasha prior to our encounter?"

"What? No... That was the first time" he shot back

"So why her? How did you choose her among all the women you know?" I asked

"She is a good friend of mine. I know a few personal things about her and that she was into wild encounters like that, and she was somewhat attracted to me. Plus, I figured that she was someone you would go for."

That last line caught me off guard. I didn't even know what that was supposed to mean. It's not like I was into women and had a type but anyway. Furthermore, he lied to me in the beginning about his marriage so I am sure he could be lying about Tasha just as easily right now.

"Do I sense a little jealousy?" he said poking me in my side, but I held a straight face which immediately wiped the smile off his.

"Did you enjoy her more than me?" I immediately felt butterflies in my stomach as I braced myself for the truth.

"Oh my God Bri? Are we really doing this?" he sighed then reached for my hands.

"I have the hots for only you. Well, you and my wife. No one else. Ok?" he awaited my response.

"But you made it seem like she was the best thing since slice bread. You spent more time with her and it was almost like I didn't exist in the room?"

"What? That is not true and you know it."

"Well you could have fooled me. The way you were all into her and so focused, it even looked like you were willing to eat her; yet you claim you don't do that."

"I cannot believe this!" he stormed in the direction of the kitchen. "I really cannot believe you are doing this. I knew this was going to happen; that is why I was hesitant about the whole idea. Briana, this was your idea," he shouted angrily while pointing at me. "This was your thing, not mine. I merely did what you wanted."

I swallowed dry and hard at the truth in his words.

"I wanted to do it, but I didn't expect you to be all up in her like that. That's all I am saying." He tossed the glass in the kitchen sink and searched frantically for his keys. "I am not doing this with you Briana," he said angrily.

Part of me understood his anger. I mean, I couldn't deny that this was my bright idea, so I had no idea why I had become so obsessed with this now. I just didn't expect him to be so enthralled with making love to another woman in my presence, and I totally miscalculated how much it would have bothered me to watch, even though I had no obligations to him.

"This is bullshit. You are ridiculous Briana. I granted your wish; now you are making me a victim. I am not here for this." He finally found his keys. "This won't be happening again with us."

"You don't need to tell me that. There will no longer be an 'us' after you walk through that door."

He looked like he had been punched in his stomach by the sound of my words.

"Really Briana. Are you fuuh…" he paused mid-sentence," still staring at me.

"It's what's best." I responded.

"You managed to figure out what is best for us amidst your craziness about a threesome?"

I couldn't respond to that because I knew fully well I was being unrealistic and irrational, but it made me feel better seeing him hurt.

"It's not just the threesome. Let's not forget that you are married." I said in my defense.

He held on to the door handle and released a gasp. "Wow Briana. Just Wow. That is the card you choose to play? You are amazing. Have it your way. I have had enough of this shit. Have a nice life." Those were his final words before he slammed the door closed behind him.

I fell to my knees. What the hell did I just do? I felt crazy and unstable. Did he really walk out on me? I bawled my eyes out and called him to apologize but he wouldn't pick up. I waited awhile and called again at a time I thought he should have been home, but still no answer. I called and called until I eventually heard a recording saying incoming calls to that number have been restricted. He must have blocked me. He was really done. I cried even more. This feeling was all too familiar. I curled up in a ball on the kitchen floor and watched my messy social life flash before my eyes. From David to Alex now Chris. I am officially tired of this emotional rollercoaster. A message came in on my phone and I grabbed it to see if it was Chris but to my disappointment, it was Alex asking if I had considered lunch. Reading the message only worsened my already foul mood.

"No I don't want to have lunch with you, not now, not ever." I texted back. I was bitter as hell. I resumed my fetal position on the floor and laid there for the rest of the night.

14

Kim

Hugh had been blowing up my phone since our lunch date, but I had refused all his offers. I was trying my best to be a faithful girlfriend to Duane and a loyal believer in Christ. But then this time around I was seriously re thinking my decisions. I knew someone like Hugh could easily put me out of my financial misery, but I am positive that I would be expected to give sex in return. I was long overdue a proper shopping day and to top it all, my business expenses were escalating. I needed a quick fix, so I did what I shouldn't have; I agreed to meet with Hugh. I was willing to take my chances with him. The aim was to flirt and tease him for a bit, fleece cash then find a way to leave without having to give myself to him. It was risky, but I felt desperate. I dressed myself in a maxi dress revealing a lot of cleavage. I realized from our last encounter that he had a thing for a lovely pair of breast.

Since I was abundantly blessed in the breast department, why not use it to my advantage?

He arrived to pick me up exactly the time he said he would have. This time he was driving a Mercedes. At the sight of this, I became excited. Maybe the Lord sent Hugh; maybe he was destined for me. I smiled even more, when I realized he was driving through an upscale community. When we arrived at his apartment, I was dumbfounded. It was nothing short of spectacular. I could see that he had refurbished it into a modern living space that was worthy of the cover of any issue of a Home & Garden Magazine. As I walked around on the hardwood floors and admired the expensive décor, I couldn't help but think that I had finally hit the jackpot. Everything about his place reeked money- right down, - to the very air I breathed.

"Your place is lovely," I tried to act nonchalant, like such luxury was not a big deal to me; but the truth was, I loved it and missed it. It was a constant struggle for me not to get excited. I don't know what it was about the combination of men and money that turned me on so much. Hugh didn't say a word at first, his piercing eyes rolling up and down my body, then back up again. Our bodies understood each other and we were definitely on the same page.

"You are lovely", he said licking his lips. Although this gesture excited me, I maintained my composure even though I was yearning to gobble him up. I knew I had to play this one right. I couldn't allow my first multibillionaire to slip through my fingers quickly, so I immediately dismissed my original plan to tease then leave. I needed to bring my best game to the plate.

I leaned over and kissed him. Without breaking the kiss, Hugh slowly made his way towards a room. His hands were already exploring my body. He was rough, but I could work with that. I lived for bedroom aggression. We kissed our way to the bedroom which was just as impressive as the other rooms in his fabulous apartment. All the furniture was mahogany and looked like something out of a movie. I decided to put on a show to really make our second encounter memorable. I was so darn good at this, I felt like I could be a stripper in another life. I stepped away from him and began swaying my hips seductively. I gripped one of the columns on the bed, wrapped my legs around it, then ran my hands along my thighs, and lingered at my sweet spot for a few seconds before gripping my girls where I stopped to pull down the top of the dress. As I stood top less jiggling my girls in front of him, he looked as though he was ready to pounce on me.

"Bring that sexy ass over here," he commanded. With a smirk on his face looking like a kid in a candy store.

I removed the entire dress and approached him bare. He buried his face in my breast and started slopping all over them. "Oh God, Yes!!" I squealed in pleasure.

He fed on my nipples like a breastfeeding child. I grabbed the back of his head pulling him closer, and then gyrated my hips even more.

"Mmmmm-I love sucking your titties." He looked up at me. I threw my head back and enjoyed the action.

130

I must admit, he really knew how to make the girls happy. The bonus question was whether he could be consistent in pleasing the kitty. Unfortunately, I wasn't going to find out. Our heads snapped towards the door when we heard what sounds like keys dangling and someone struggling to get in.

"Shittt!!" he said in a panicked whisper, and in one quick movement, he shoved me from his lap and jumped up. " SHIT, SHIT..that's my wife...why is she home..shit shit." I was in his bedroom, buck ass naked and he was acting like a scared little bitch. This was not a part of the plan. I didn't even know the bastard was married. There was no way a woman could whip my ass. I was ready for her. I didn't know what he was scared about anyway. Hugh tried to shove me under the bed, but I resisted. There was no way in hell I was going to hide from his punk ass wife under the bed. I am a bad bitch. He became even more flustered. "Does she look like she carries a nine millimeter hand gun on her person all the time and is not afraid to use it?" he asked as he started scrambling to hide the evidence.

" *Ahh hell naw. This woman is crazy.*" I thought as my heart went into overdrive. What on earth was I supposed to do now? I was thinking of hiding in one of the other bedrooms but that idea went down the drain when Hugh's dumb ass quickly scooped up my clothes and shoved them under the bed.

"Why the hell did you do that?"

131

"Kim we have no time to argue." He turned to me. "Get in the closet. I will distract her or something so you can leave but PLEASE be quiet." He pointed towards the closet. Without putting up a fight, I rushed over there and closed it quickly behind me. I stooped in the closet and tried to control the rush of adrenaline that suddenly consumed me. I peeked through the blinds as his wife strolled into the bedroom and found him there. Hugh had propped himself on the bed, leaning back on his elbows. They were having a cute little conversation about their day at work and he asked why she was home before the usual time. It was somewhat sweet of him to allow his wife to recite her day. Most men were usually not interested in such things, but at least he tried to seem like he cared, even if it may not have been genuine. It was not a bad conversation but I stopped paying attention at the point when I felt something cold and rough fall on my shoulders. I jumped and nearly choked myself to death by trying not to scream. The urge was definitely there. Hugh grabbed his wife and immediately plastered her with kisses. I suppose he heard the rumblings coming from the closet.

I slapped the thing off my shoulders. "What the fu..." a god damn lizard. Looking at the lizard on floor across from me gave me chills. Worst part was, there was nothing I could do about it.

I rechanneled my mind to the action on the other side of the closet to help me conquer my fear of being so close to a lizard that refused to move. Lord knows how badly I wanted to scream. I contemplated making a run for it but then the thought of being shot in the ass by his wife overshadowed my initial plan. This was an opportunity for me to scrutinize his wife- an out of shape woman in her fifties. She took off her shirt and exposed the soggiest pair of breasts I had ever seen. Suddenly, the bastard had a smirk on his face; the same smirk he just had after viewing my voluptuous girls. That's when it dawned on me that these bastards were about to have sex. He was supposed to get rid of this bitch and free me from the closet, but no, instead he was about to sex her flabby ass. I wanted to jump out the closet and smack the hell out of Hugh.

How could he be so disgusting? Just moments ago he was sucking on my plump young titties like he was recovering from a famine. I was pretty sure some of my juices were on his hands. I watched as he stripped down to expose an awful pear shaped body that highlighted his age. I must have been blind-sided by our first encounter or maybe it was the fact that he took me shopping, but I didn't pay keen attention to his body until now. I couldn't remember ever seeing a scrotal sack hanging as low as his. All the money in the world couldn't conceal the fact that this was one unattractive man once his clothes were off. How embarrassing.

As I watched Hugh and his wife, my stomach churned at how mundane their lovemaking was. First of all, they stuck to the played out missionary position. His wife was stiff as a board, and he gave about eight humps before he was squealing like he had just bust the best nut ever known to man. They were both panting like they had just finished a marathon of sex. That was five minutes tops! I was appalled by how boring he now appeared in bed. He definitely wouldn't be able to tame my kitty. But this wasn't an issue; I was not about to lose out. I had my eyes on the prize no matter what. His wife kissed him then said she was going to take a quick shower. That was my cue. I watched as her wrinkled, freckled tatted ass strolled into the bathroom. I then quickly but quietly emerged from the closet and not a moment too soon either because that damn lizard was working on my nerves.

Hugh shot me a look of terror as I emerged from the closet. "Kim what are you doing?" he whispered looking nervously towards the bathroom door.

"What your bitch ass should have done all this time. I need to get out of here, and I will require compensation to stroll out here quietly" I said, wasting no time securing what I initially came here for anyway. After what I was just forced to endure, I would make this worth my time.

"Kim, get dressed and leave please," he begged. I laughed. "Kim, just go," he begged even more. This man was really terrified of his wife, but I on the other hand was slightly turned on by the possibilities of getting caught. He pulled my clothes from beneath the bed and shoved them towards me.

I stood firm even after receiving my clothes. "I need to be compensated," I said once more. He looked at me with pleading eyes. I held a straight face.

"Seriously Kim?" he shook his head. I remained resolute. He reached for his pants that were on the floor, pulled out his bill fold and removed a five thousand dollar bill.

"I am going to need more than that," I protested. After a defeated sigh, "how much more?" he asked. "I need everything that's in the wallet." He looked like he was about to protest until we heard the shower stop. He panicked once more. He pulled five more five thousand dollar bills from his billfold and threw it in my hand. That was thirty thousand in total. I didn't sit well with that figure. Anything in 30's reminded me of the son of a bitch who infected me with herpes. I needed more. "This is still not enough", I stood waiting with my hands on my hip.

"Oh my God Kimberly," he squealed with a horrified look on his face.

"Did you say something honey?" his wife shouted from the bathroom.

"I am on the phone dear'" he responded with his eyes still fixed on the bathroom door. He looked like he was about to have diarrhea. He opened the drawer of the night stand, dug in and pulled out a thick wad of cash. He was shaking after he forked it over. "Just go," he whispered, defeated.

His wife helped me out more than she ever knew. I think I need to be trapped in a closet more often. I laughed at the thought.

He shoved me out the room, still eyeing the bathroom. "Get out of here," he said motioning with his hand. By the time I made it to the front door, I managed to slip into my dress. I clutched my cash tightly as I rushed out of the apartment. I ran down the stairs then paused to count my stash. That's when I realized how generous Hugh had been. My expenses were covered and I was now able to put some money into my little restaurant and still had a generous bonus remaining for my troubles. I jiggled my booty and did a little dance after realizing I had earned close to two hundred thousand dollars in a couple of minutes. I remained in the parking lot for a few minutes putting on my footwear while trying to figure out what my next move was. I wasn't familiar with the area so I didn't know how to get out. It seemed like I would have to call a cab which I am sure would be extremely expensive. I didn't want to use any of the money I just obtained on paying a cab. Further more, I didn't even know the name of the community so what would I tell the cab company? I sat on the wall and made myself comfortable. I decided to wait to see if his wife would leave soon seeing that she wasn't supposed to have been home. I hid behind the branches of a tree and watched closely as people traversed in and out the apartment. Maybe that was a sign from God, because I was bound to have sex with Hugh had his wife not show up.

I was contemplating my next move. What if I waited for Hugh then he took back the cash from me or hurt me or something. Maybe it wasn't such a good idea to wait for him. I took out my phone, turned on my GPS and tapped into google maps to find out where exactly I was, but as soon as the results were generated, my phone battery died. Could my day get any worst? So I decided to walk the distance we travelled. It was a mighty long walk but I was out of options.

As I made my journey, I felt extremely embarrassed. The things I go through for money. Why was I like that? This love for money was more than just a demon. Initially, I was concerned about Hugh taking the money from me not even thinking about the dangers of walking back to civilization by myself. Maybe I was paranoid but I could feel the stares of passersby piercing my back. I guess it was absurd to see someone walking in the vicinity. I took my own sweet time and prayed that God protected me, though I felt undeserving of his mercies at this moment. There were no off roads to this community. It was one way in and one way out, so I knew the chances of getting lost was slim. I busied my thoughts with moments I spent with Bri, my business and just about everything that made me happy, in order to ease my mind off the journey ahead. I walked for almost half hour and still there was no indication that I was close. One passerby stopped and volunteered a ride but I refused. I kept my mind occupied and continued walking. About 10 minutes later, to my surprise, Hugh stopped at my feet. I was somewhat elated to see him but for a brief moment I thought about the money I fleeced but then desperation for a ride prevailed. I hopped in and made myself comfortable. I exhaled a long sigh of relief.

"After all the money you stole from me, you couldn't spend on a cab?"

"My battery died."

"Conveniently." He said as a matter of fact.

I needed a quick come back so I focused on the issue at hand.

"So you never mentioned that you were married?"

"It never came up, and I didn't think it mattered."

"You didn't think it mattered? So you cheat on your wife all the time then?"

"No..I didn't mean it that way."

"I am sure."

"Look can we start over now that you know my little secret?"

I shifted in my seat as I thought about the question. I supposed I could earn a couple more hundred thousand dollars before calling it quits.

"I will think about it."

"After you pocketed my 150g, you are telling me you are going to think about it? Do you think it's fair to take that much money then cut ties with the individual?"

My throat became a little dry, as he hit me with the truth. He made a valid point but unfortunately I had no answers. He looked at me once more then pulled over the vehicle. By this point, I could hear my heart pounding in my chest. If this man was about to kill me, I couldn't blame him. I didn't move a muscle as I eagerly anticipated his next move. My body was as stiff as a board. He switched off the engine then placed one hand on my leg.

"Kim, I like you and I want us to get closer. If it doesn't work out then I will let you be but give us a try. You know I can give you the world and by the look of things, I know you don't mind that life. So what do you say?"

I fidgeted a bit before giving a response.

"Ok, I will give it a try."

He then placed gentle kisses along my neck and worked his way up to my lips. I was still tense but I returned the gesture. He placed one last kiss on my nose before switching on the ignition.

"Bank or home?"

I looked at him puzzled.

"Are you going to deposit the money you obtained or should I take you home?

I wondered if this was a trick question. Then again, he had the opportunity to kill me and he didn't, not to mention how he could have driven past me or taken some form of revenge for what I did to him. The aftermath could have been worst, so I was grateful.

"Bank it is," I finally responded. He dropped me off then waited for me in the car while I conducted business. The bank was surprisingly empty, so I was out of there and on my way home in a matter of minutes.

Upon arriving home, we kissed once more before departing our separate ways.

15

Briana

The next few weeks were really a drag. I felt sad and lonely after the ordeal with Chris. To make matters worse, he made no attempt to contact me. I suppose now would be a good time to clear him out of my system. Everything happens for a reason was what I told myself. After all, Chris was married. It's not like he had intentions of leaving his wife any time soon, and I didn't want that either. But I didn't mind the fact that he filled that void of not having a man any at all in my life. Sharing someone's partner was way better than being single. At least you had someone to go on dates with or to comfort you occasionally. But I had to face the harsh reality that Chris was gone and move on with my life. This left me in a funky mood most times, so my conversations with Steve were not as fulfilling as how we started out. Most times I didn't respond to his messages on time because I was afraid that I might unintentionally snap at him and push him away and he seemed like such a good guy. I wanted to get to know him, but I just wasn't in the right frame of mind to do that anytime soon. But then when he asked me out on a dinner date for the third time in one week and totaled the umpteenth time in Lord knows how many weeks, I finally agreed. I really thought he would have lost interest by now but he pursued me regardless. I felt somewhat guilty for the way I ignored him, so I tried my best to look very sexy. Plus, it had been a while since I had gotten dolled up too. Most days, I have only been traveling to and from work. So tonight's dinner date was a nice little break for me. I was low key excited to be honest. I gave myself one final look in the mirror before I left. On my way to the restaurant, Steve called to say he was running a little late but had already made reservations. He told me to go ahead and choose a nice seat to dine.

Upon arrival, I contemplated waiting in the car. I didn't want to be sitting alone at the table, especially since he didn't mention how late he would be. What if I ended up waiting for an half hour? I couldn't imagine the servers checking with me every minute making sure everything was ok; they probably thought that my date stood me up? These days' men made me so paranoid. I couldn't help but overthink the simplest of things in relation to men.

I waited for about 10 minutes in the car before going inside. I decided that I would have left if he hadn't called or arrived within twenty minutes. But thankfully he showed up five minutes later and took me out of misery.

"I am so sorry for being late. I can never leave my office without someone calling me the moment I'm headed through the door." I watched him put his cellphone on silent as he said that. He then looked at me politely and told me thanks for accepting his dinner invite.

"I must say I became a little worried because our conversations seemed to have changed drastically. I reread every text message and reminisced on every phone call, just to see if I had said something offensive that may have pushed you away. Because I just couldn't understand why you had become so unresponsive and turned down all my lunch invites."

"I am sorry. I have been going through a rough patch and just needed some time alone."

"Understood, but please do me a favour? If you should ever go through another rough patch, please tell me you need to be alone and I will give you your space rather than have me thinking that I did something wrong. It's not a nice feeling."

"Look at you being sensitive," I said.

"I will try to be open with you next time."

"Thank you." He said. I could tell he was reassured.

"Are you sure you won't be missing any important calls?" I asked, highlighting the fact that he silenced his phone.

"I try not to let work interfere with my home life. So whenever I had company, I try to dedicate myself solely to them."

"Your family must be lucky" I said.

"My parents were busy individuals, and I don't think I had ever had a conversation with them without one of them answering the phone or flying out the door. My mother was a surgeon and my father was a pediatrician and still is, in a small town in Oshawa. He is still practicing and going strong."

"This sounded like a nice way to grow up. But if your family is in Canada, how did you wind up here?"

"I came to Jamaica to work on a project and I fell in love with it. So I decided to purchase a home here, but I travel a lot just the same but mainly to the States and the Caribbean. But I get more work done when I am here in JA. I can't explain why; it is what it is. I simply just love what I do."

"Which was what?" I was intrigued. I wondered if he could tell.

"A network engineer." He was easy to talk to and we only paused long enough to order dinner.

"A Caesar salad and a chicken quesadilla." We both looked at the menu and ordered the same thing in unison. We both chuckled at this.

"What is your job description?"

"I am a nurse/midwife. Just like you, I love what I do, but sometimes I questioned my career choice when the workload becomes overwhelming. Sometimes working the emergency department and the labour ward simultaneously is hectic but I suppose I make it work."

"Nice. Sounds very stressful. How is your boyfriend dealing with that?"

I smiled. "You sure don't hesitate to find out information."

"I mean, that's why we are here right...to know each other a bit more?"

"There is no boyfriend to deal with my hectic work schedule, but I do hope to commit to a family and my career one day."

"How long have you been single?"

"A few weeks." I said dryly not wanting to talk too much about that.

"Oh..That explains the rough patch."

"Mhhm..What about you. How does your spouse or children handle you traveling so often? How old are your kids? My gut response is always twelve and five"

He laughed before answering the question. "I've been divorced for twenty years. I travel a lot as I mentioned earlier, so I haven't been able to find that person who understands and accepts my work ethic. My daughter is twenty-three and is getting a masters degree in social work in Canada at the moment."

"That's nice. You must be a proud dad."

"You bet.

The food arrived, and we continued talking while we ate. We covered a variety of subjects, and I was fascinated by how modest he was despite his very important job. I liked how direct and unassuming he was and to top it off he made me laugh.

"So do you live with your family?"

"No. I live alone. My mother died when I was 12 and my father, well I don't know where or who he is. I grew up with a friend of the family and by the time I got to college, I was pretty much on my own. I had a little apartment that I rented during that time until I finished school and was able to buy my house."

"Wow. That is very impressive. You seem to have accomplished a great deal and you are so young. People my age are still working to obtain what you have. That's fantastic. I love when young people are ambitious. Keep it up."

I think I like Steve. He was definitely open with me and much warmer than I expected, and we were both surprisingly forthcoming with each other though he was twice my age.

"So what were you like as a kid or teen?"

"I was shy, fat and had buckteeth until I had my braces." I said with a modest smile.

He burst out in laughter before adding, "And then you turned into a swan."

I blushed at what he said.

I glanced up and realized that servers were clearing the tables; that's when we both looked at our watches and realized how late it was. We had been talking for hours; yet, I felt like I could keep talking to him all night. I regretted that we had to part. Steve paid for the meals and we walked out of the restaurant together.

"Thank you for meeting with me for dinner tonight," he said sincerely, as he walked me to my car. "I am certainly glad I met a young woman like you. Maybe we can do it again sometime?"

"Most definitely," I said smiling. "Thanks again for dinner," I said and waved as I drove away. I was pleasantly surprised at how easy and fun it had been dining with him. He hadn't disappointed me in any way.

****

Steve and I had gone on several dates since our first dinner date. Even though we both had busy schedules, we made a commitment to see each other at least three times for the week and that we did. Every Tuesday and Thursday were date nights. The weekends were always flexible but I reserved that for quality time with the girls. After all, I was a religious supporter of Kim's Wings Fiesta on Fridays. Plus, I hadn't told her about Steve as yet. I don't even think I mentioned that Chris and I broke it off, and I am sure she would not have been bothered by this, because she was never a fan of him. Who's to tell, if she wasn't responsible for praying for us to grow apart seeing that our relationship was adulterous. But, I promised myself that I would have updated her after tonight's date night.

Steve and I were about to watch Sleepless with Jamie Foxx. Although I was not a fan of Jamie Foxx, I went along without complaint, because it was his choice. It was his company that mattered. I don't know why, but I always felt like a kid at a birthday party in his presence. There was never a dull moment around him. He had a way of making me feel welcome and at ease and as though we knew each other better than we did. He reserved box seats and these were excellent. As soon as we sat down, he offered to get me hot dogs and a drink, but I decided to go with him and we chatted along the way.

"Do you come to the movies often?" I asked smiling at him as we joined the queue of one of the concession stands with dozens of other people.

"Not really, only when there is a good action movie out. I don't mind it, but it is not a favourite pass time of mine. What I do enjoy is a day at the beach or maybe I should say, a day on the sand because I never swim."

We both laughed.

"Just soaking up the sun with a drink in hand and watching sexy women in bikini was good enough for me."

"Understood. Well maybe we need a beach day one weekend then."

"Hint noted," he said as he ordered food for what seemed like he was about to feed the whole theatre. Nachos with cheese, 2 jumbo hot dogs, chicken nuggets, 1 large bucket of popcorn and two extra-large orange juices with a bottle of water.

It's a good thing I decided to accompany him or else I don't know how he would have transported all this food on his own.

"Don't worry, I will have whatever you don't want. But I like to have it all, so I don't need to get anything during intermission. I'd rather just be able to watch the movie, eat my heart out and be merry. I can't afford to miss anything."

"You are too funny," I said shaking my head in disbelief at his rationale for buying all that food.

"Do you like mustard, ketchup, mayonnaise, relish or pickles?" he asked as he stuffed a wad of paper napkins in his pocket. "Mustard and ketchup please." He grabbed them at the next concession booth as we made our way back to our seats. We indulged in the food before the movie started and chatted in between. We sure could talk.

The story line of the movie got off to a slow start. Thankfully, by the time we had gotten to intermission, we were completely taken up with how action packed and interesting it was. The food was also half way. I was surprised at how I was chowing it all down. Moving from popcorn, to chicken nuggets to my hot dogs. At one point, Steve glanced at me, and I gave myself a little reality check. I felt a little embarrassed that I was acting gluttonous.

"Don't be shy; eat your heart out," he said as if to reassure me that he wasn't being judgmental. By the end of the movie, there was nothing but napkins and paper cups remaining. We devoured it all. The movie turned out to be good as well. I was in shock when he suggested that we go for ice cream after the movies. The sound of it made me nauseous. I had no room for nothing else, so he passed on the thought and took me home instead.

We kissed good night before I exited his vehicle and entered my home. God, why did he have to be so sexy and sweet? Why hadn't he messed up yet, so that I could find a reason to be turned off? He was turning my world upside down, but I didn't want to fall like a ton of bricks for another man; it was too soon. But it seemed to be happening anyway and all I could do was try to put the brakes on and slow it down, if I couldn't stop it. He was just too perfect. The minute I closed the door, I dialed Kim.

"What's up Heifer?" she answered. "Nothing much. Just got back from the movies"

"Ugh..Let me guess, you and Chris?"

"No..We broke up."

"We what...?" she repeated in disbelief then immediately added a hallelujah. Now that's more of the response I expected.

"I went out with Steve."

"So Steve is the new man?"

"Not really. We have gone out a few times, but there is no relationship title to it; just friends. He is really nice though. I like him."

"Aww... I am happy for you hun. Welcome to the human race. I can't wait to meet the guy who seduced the virgin queen."

"Don't get too excited. I haven't slept with him as yet. We are having a nice time. There is no need to rush into anything."

"Of course, you would say that. You always take a long time to give it up. Briana, dead people have sex more often than you do. You should drink more or smoke a joint or something."

"Will you shut up," I said dying with laughter. Kim was too much; I just can't with her at times but I loved her. She was always so entertaining.

"So when will I meet this new guy?"

"Maybe he can come to Wings Fiesta tomorrow? What you think?"

"That sounds good. Actually, that's perfect. That way if I don't like him I can burn him with hot oil or something."

"Oh my gosh....Girl bye. I can't with you. You better be on your best behavior and not intimidate my future husband."

"Oh...so you won't own him as a boyfriend, but you are claiming husband title? But look at you, get them goodie."

"Good Night Kimberly. Make sure them chicken wings be on point tomorrow or else...."

"Mwah...Night Bri."

16

Kim

That morning I woke up in an awful mood. I didn't sleep well the night before, because I kept experiencing shooting pains in my buttocks coupled with a mixture of a tingling and dull throbbing pain in my vagina. I knew that it was only a matter of time before the sores would appear; this was an inconvenient time, because I was completely out of my medication. I tend to experience these symptoms whenever I was about to have a herpes flare, especially if I became stressed. I only hoped that it didn't present itself as badly as it did the last time. I grabbed a few ice packs from the refrigerator then wrapped it neatly in a towel. Laying on the bed, I placed it on my vagina and held it in place for about 30 minutes. This soothed the symptoms to some extent. I didn't have much time in my schedule to visit a doctor today, so I really hoped the symptoms subsided. If Briana had been made aware of my situation, getting medications would have been so much easier. But this type of information I didn't feel comfortable telling anyone else, other than my doctor. To show the extent of my paranoia, I made sure to visit a doctor out of town that I didn't think Briana knew since medicine was her niche and her connections in this context were strong.

I could only imagine how disappointed she would have been with me if she ever found out about this. Especially since she lectured me back in the day, multiple times, on the importance of safe sex. That which I clearly lied about. What you don't know won't hurt you, was one of my mantras, and I was sticking to it. I replaced my ice packs in the refrigerator, got dressed then headed to the basic school for my daily lunch duties. By the time my duties were done, I went to use the ladies room when I noticed the blisters were out in their numbers. I had to call Hugh immediately and reschedule our lunch date. I knew the main thing on the agenda was sex, lunch was just to sweeten the labour. My vagina needed medical attention urgently. So now, I was left with no other choice but to visit the doctor. A task that usually takes the whole day. The world and their mother seemed to visit this particular doctor. No matter what time of the day you arrived or even how early you arrived, the office was always full. Other doctors are usually on duty as well, but every-one preferred the same doctor, myself included. If the majority fluctuated to the one man, why should I then be the one to deviate?

I texted Hugh the whole time I was at the doctor's office. It was still an early stage in our relationship. Although, I didn't officially give him an answer, I could already tell that he was the type of person who believed that he should always have things his way. He made it clear that he wasn't pleased about why I had cancelled our lunch date. Even though I explained that I wasn't feeling well, according to him, it couldn't be anything that sex couldn't fix. I don't know where he derived his theories, but sex, in his opinion, was the most magical thing in his repertoire. If you had a headache, backache, bellyache, felt lazy or moody, sex was apparently the answer. You would think someone who worshipped sex so much would have mind-blowing, toe curling, and bedroom tongue speaking abilities? I was fortunate if I even got 10 minutes of pleasure out of him at any one time. The old fart would nut in minutes all the time, but it was the money that kept me sane. Hugh was my jackpot, and I wasn't letting him go that easily. He offered to keep my company at the doctor's office and although this wasn't necessary, I agreed because I knew it would give him peace of mind. He just needed reassurance that my reason for cancelling our time together was because I was out with some other dude. He was so easy to read.

And I was right. When he arrived, he spent about 10 minutes with me before he left, stating that he had other things to do. I made sure to collect the money for the doctor's visit from him plus extras to fill the prescription, since he needed to keep tabs on me. After he left, that was the last of his text messages.

The wait at the office was really long. By the time I got through, it would have been during the time of Wings Fiesta's staging, so I instructed my assistants and basically left them in charge for the night. I told mommy to oversee things until I arrived. When I eventually left the doctor's office, it was well after 6. By the time I arrived home, it was almost 8.

My first stop in the house was the kitchen, just to make sure things were in place. I had never before left anyone in charge of the business, but they were doing a good job. In fact, I ended up leaving them to finish up while I spent the night relaxing with my clique: Briana, Anastasia and Bugz. To be honest, I felt weary from the long wait to see the doc then having to travel home, but I managed to muster enough energy to play several rounds of dominoes with my friends. I paused occasionally to check on things which were still going smoothly. At least until the conniving little heifer named Keisha decided to create a scene. She pretty much deliberately smashed several liquor bottles, then pretentiously staggered around the area she had been seated, knocking over the chairs, while her friends all laughed and watched her make an ass of herself. This was all a part of her plan to provoke me. She then staggered over to my table then swiped all the dominoes to the floor. She was lucky that the angels on my shoulders, Briana and Anastasia, were present; and the fact that she acted out in my place of business because otherwise, Bugz and I were ready to beat her down. This woman worked on my nerves. I knew fully well she wasn't drunk. This wasn't over though. I was way too petty to let this incident slide. She may have won this round, but revenge is best served cold. I promised her that I would retaliate when she least expected it.

"Damn fool," I said hissing my teeth before walking away to calm the adrenaline pumping through my body.

"What was that about?" Bri asked as she approached me in the kitchen.

"She is just stupid," I said angrily, throwing down the utensils on the counter. "She is flipping out because her man wants me more than her."

"Gosh Kim, I thought we were over these games."

"I am not playing any games but clearly she wants to. Her man passed by one day at school during lunch break to give his son something and she must have caught us apparently having too good of a conversation and interpreted that as flirting. Mind you, we exchanged numbers but it has been a very casual friendship since. That very first encounter was very innocent and nothing more than a friendly conversation. Since then, she has been acting up whenever she ran into me in public spaces. She best believe she just messed with the wrong person. An attempt to trash my event Briana? Really? Just wait till I get her."

"Let it go Kim. Be the bigger person. Keisha is always like that anyway. She loves attention."

"Oh you know her too?"

"Not really, but she is a regular patient at one of my medical centres, and she behaves the same way-always craving attention. I am not fond of her either because she has no manners."

"You said she is a patient of yours?" I said looking back at Briana with a sly look.

"No....no Kim. Whatever you are thinking, I won't be a part of it."

I guess the look on my face made her edgy. "You don't even know what I want."

"No I don't, and I think we should keep it that way."

"Come on Bri...please. I promise it won't be anything crazy."

"Let me hear what's on your mind?"

"Can you give me her number?"

"What?? No..I can't do that"

"Why not? What harm could I possibly do with a phone number? If I said address, then there would be cause for concern..."

Briana looked as if she was thinking through the possibilities.

"Why do you need her contact then?"

"I don't know yet but I am sure I will figure it out eventually."

"No Kim. I don't like the sound of this. Something isn't right. What you are asking me to do is so wrong. That's violating confidentiality."

"Bri..Don't sweat it. Who will know that you gave it to me?"

"I don't like the sound of this Kim. I don't want to be caught in whatever scheme you are deriving."

"You won't. I promise. I won't do anything to get you in trouble. And if by some miraculous reason, it should come up, I could easily say I got her number from her man's phone. After all, she thinks we are screwing so; might as well"

"Umm no. You are going to leave that man alone Kim. Satisfy with Duane."

"Duane is too much of a Christian."

"And you should be too," she said smacking me on the arms.

"I am trying, but the temptations are just too much."

"Spend more time with Duane, maybe some of his goodly Christian mentality will rub off on you."

As much as I hated hearing it, she may have been right. Duane was such a sweetheart.

"I will try harder. So you will get the number for me though?" I asked Bri once more.

"This conversation never happened," she said exiting the kitchen.

I did my usual rounds and pre clean up until all the activities came to an end.

****

I was having a late lunch with Duane at Fromage when my cell vibrated, and I ignored it. But if Duane didn't change this topic of me not attending church as often as I used to, I was bound to use these phone calls as my scapegoat to getting out of what felt like reprimand. The truth is, I didn't think church was compatible with my schedule anymore. God was taking too long to make certain things happen, and I was running out of patience and would get worked up unnecessarily. I tried my best to manage my moods and stress levels because the moment I become overwhelmed, this only resulted in me experiencing prodromal herpes symptoms, which was not only uncomfortable but it also interrupted my cash influx. If I can't give up the cookie then there is no compensation. These last days Duane spent more time ministering to me, rather than treating me like his girlfriend. He was definitely one of those goodly Christians; one of those

161

sweet dark chocolate delight, with the sexiest lips and pearly white teeth. To say he was handsome was an understatement. His chocolate ass was fine as hell. I stopped counting how many times I committed fornication in my mind with this man. I yearned for his chocolate hose to put out my flames, but he never touched me inappropriately-not once. I loved him though, and I really wanted our relationship to prosper. He, on the other hand, was way too advanced in this spiritual journey to even qualify as equally yoked with someone like myself. But I was still hopeful.

"Baby, is it your friends who are distracting you from the house of the Lord?"

"No honey, I just think I need a break from the church. I need some time to recollect my thoughts and to figure myself out." I said. That was the best excuse I could come up with.

"But you don't have to break from the church to do that. We can help you figure yourself out. It is better when you have the love and support of spiritual warriors. It would make the process easier, and I am sure it would also be less distracting to you. We have all gone through these phases. We have all had similar moments to what you are now experiencing. Let us help you Kim?" he pleaded with me.

My phone vibrated once more and saved the day. "Duane, give me a minute, I need to take this call." I said.

"Do your thing baby. I love to see you going." He smiled, as I rose from the table and walked towards the front door. I hit the talk button on my phone then cooed into my Bluetooth.

"Dean baby, how yah doing?" the minute I heard his voice. I knew exactly what he wanted. Dean was next in line on my list of sponsors. I needed additional chairs, tables, cooking utensils and a new sound system to improve the next staging of Wings Fiesta. I also wanted revenge against his girl who created a scene at the last staging of my event. Hitting me up proved that he was just as ready to be put into rotation.

"I want to see you. I need to see you. Stop playing games and bring your ass to me," he said.

"You are putting me off to be with your church boyfriend. You know I can give you so much more than what he has to offer. I will take care of you the way you deserve."

"Look Dean, I am not exclusive to anyone, so don't be thinking once we hook up, we have somehow become a thing...ok..,,just so we are clear."

"B..stop sweating it. I know this. Remember I have my woman, so you don't even have to worry about that."

"You sure about that? Because once I lay it on you, I promise you, it can become like a bad habit. A very expensive habit at that." I waited to see if he would protest but his silence was confirmation that he didn't mind spending on women.

"So will you be giving me that sweet ass today? I have a room at The Rex hotel. Meet me there in twenty minutes."

"I can't. I haven't even gotten to the food yet with Duane."

"You need to ditch that nigga, and let me blow your mind, baby girl." I immediately saw dollar signs. Let's see how much Dean was willing to give.

"I don't know Dean, Duane was willing to assist me with purchasing furniture for my event, so I don't want to mess that up," I said dropping the bait. Sometimes it amazed me how well I could lie.

"Assist you with purchasing furniture? With his chump change? Kim if you ditch this guy right now, I will purchase the furniture for you and even supply all the meat that you may need. As a matter of fact, I could supply you with groceries for a month."

"I will hit you up when I am there," I said without hesitation. I walked back to the table regretting what I was about to do, but I was a practical woman and needed to handle my business at all times.

"I am sorry Duane but there is something I need to sort out. Is it possible for us to reschedule this lunch date? I am really sorry I ruined the moment" I said with feigned regret. The disappointment on his face almost stirred up a little emotion in me, but I quickly dismissed it. I kept my eyes on the prize. I hugged him then exchanged a few kisses before leaving. As I exited the restaurant, I kept it cute in the event Duane was still watching, and I was almost sure he was, so I had to put on a little show with my booty that I was sure would entertain him and maybe even catch a few additional eyes. I was always seeking new prey. The moment I entered a taxi, I sent Dean a text message telling him I was on my way.

Fifteen minutes later, I arrived at the Rex hotel. I called Dean for the room number but decided to spend a few minutes in the ladies room to freshen up before heading up to see him. While fixing my lip balm, the devil on my shoulder gave me a marvelous idea. I think I may use Keisha's number a bit earlier than I expected. I promised Briana that I wouldn't do anything stupid or anything that would lead back to her, so I am sure she would most definitely approve of my big idea. This was payback to Keisha without even getting physical. I smiled as I walked toward the elevator. This smile became fixed as I became excited about what was about to transpire. As I approached the room, I dialed Keisha's number. As soon as she answered, I recognized her voice immediately and said, "whatever you do, don't hang up! I am about to teach you a valuable lesson on who not to mess with." I knocked on the door. "Dean, honey, open up," I said.

"Dean honey? Who the hell is this?" Keisha's voice sounded panic –stricken.

"Is your boy hard and ready for me baby?" I asked sweetly as Dean opened the door and stepped aside to make way for me to enter. I flipped my hair over my shoulders, making sure it covered the wireless earpiece through which Keisha would still be able to hear everything.

" Damn woman you look so juicy. I would spread you on a platter and devour you right now." He greeted which set off a tirade of expletives in my ear. I knew for sure that I had Keisha's undivided attention by now and I sure knew how to host a show. I put on some dramatics and shuddered with excitement.

"Well grab your cutlery and enjoy baby. I am all yours." Dean stepped closer reaching for me but I lifted my hand like a crossing guard stopping traffic. "Did you forget about my groceries as promised?" I said jumping straight to business."

"Hell no babe; I am a man of my word. Stop sweating." He reached in his pocket and handed me a fistful of bills. I didn't even bother to count it. I just stuffed the money in my bag. The last thing I was worried about was him shorting me.

"Now are you ready to enjoy the ride?" Dean asked as he unbuttoned his shirt and flexed his huge muscles. I really liked men with nicely chiseled bodies; but truthfully, muscle bound guys wasn't a thing for me. Once you had a big upper body, it was a slight turn off. Besides they always seemed to be lacking in the performance area, probably due to all those steroids they are known for pumping. After all, I had a very low tolerance for men who were not able to provide me sexual gratification.

"Well before we go any further, let us just make sure we are on the same page. First and foremost, I will only go down on you, if you go down on me." I shifted my head from side to side and tried to hold my composure as Keisha would not stop screaming in my earpiece. "I loved to be bent over and pounded from behind, grabbing my breast, hair, neck, just about anything you feel like grabbing."

At this point, I think Keisha was about to lose her damn mind. I remained focused on the task at hand, which was more about pissing her off than it was about sexual gratification. "Please know that if you go anywhere near the booty hole, you better be ready to go buy a whole restaurant for me to operate my business, cause it's going to cost you." I folded my arms over my chest and asked him, "do you think you can handle that?"

"Bend over and find out." We both laughed at his little joke but his girlfriend sure as hell wasn't finding this amusing.

"This heifer cannot be talking to my man; to my Dean!" she protested. I had no doubt she knew damn well that it was her precious man getting ready to give me good sex, and I was sure ready to enjoy every second of it. I felt relieved already, knowing that when I was done here with Dean, she would probably be heart broken. I was about to get this bitch back for ruining my event. Now she knows not to mess with me in the future. And the wad of five thousand dollar bills in my purse was a nice little bonus for all my troubles.

"Are you ready to enjoy the ride baby?" I asked again just to make sure Keisha heard it a second time.

"Oh yes babe, I have been wanting you to ride me since I saw you that day at school. I want to spank that ass and nibble on your girls" He said with eyes fixed on the prize. I approached him and pressed my whole body against him.

"Mmmm. I like the sound of that." He grabbed a handful of my breast. I released a moan. I wished I had adjusted the volume on my earpiece before I called this crazy woman. She was screaming so much I thought I might end up with hearing loss.

I stepped back and unzipped my dress, giving Dean full view of my birthday suit. His eyes looked like they were ready to pop from his head at the sight. I stood in place as I awaited some form of verbal reaction.

"Th-they're as lovely as I imagined" he managed to stutter as he stood there mesmerized.

I moved the pillows from the head of the bed and arranged them the way I needed. I stretched across the pillows with my pelvic area slightly elevated and spread my legs. Dean crawled between my thighs with eyes fixed on the spot like it was made of gold. "Let me introduce you to the best place on earth." I said patting my vagina.

"The best place on earth, he mocked. It looked like the best place in the universe to me." He planted warm wet kisses on the inside of my thighs. I released yet another moan.

"Suck on it Dean," I said eagerly anticipating his tongue. "I will nurture this clit with my tongue honey, just wait for it." He murmured.

"This cannot be my Dean. He doesn't even do oral sex." She actually sounded like she was close to tears in spite of trying to act tough. She clearly didn't know her man very well because by the way he was acting with me he seemed to love going downtown. Dean buried his face between my lips.

"SSSSSSss. Yes!" I purred. When he used his fingers to separate my vagina lips and reveal my swollen clit, I just about wanted to do a play by play for his girl who claims he doesn't have skills. I was in for a treat, when Dean did this move with his tongue that took my breath away. He drilled his tongue into me, then sucked in my clit, holding it between his lips.

"Oh God!! Oh God Dean!" I cheered. After he repeated that move a few times, I came so hard. I am sure my screams could be heard on the next floor. I put my arms on my head in an attempt to recover. Maybe I should stop stereotyping against muscle bound guys because Dean just shattered my theory.

"Now, it's your turn. Bring that pretty penis over here. I bet you didn't know I was on a liquid diet?" I actually had to stifle a laugh when I heard the way Keisha began to hyperventilate. Dean eased off the bed and dropped his shorts and boxer brief. His penis wasn't huge, but it sure as hell was curved. It almost looked like a hockey stick. His rod was even harder when I deep throated him in one smooth move. I looked straight into his eyes as I tried to suck the life from him. He grabbed the back of my head moving me back and forth, I tightened my grip around his muscle.

"Jeeeeeesss-suss. God damn Kim-berrrrrly." The moment he uttered my name I heard Keisha screamed in the earpiece at the revelation. "You little whore, wait till I see you." I wasn't bothered by that comment. Surprisingly, the fact that she could hear us made my vagina even wetter. It was almost like she was actually there and watching. Plus, I had been known to enjoy giving a performance or two in my lifetime. The more turned on I became, the harder I sucked.

"Oh yes baby, suck it..Yes..suck it baby..."

Superhead didn't have shit on me I thought, as I cheered myself on while trying to stifle another laughter in the mix. I felt an explosion happening soon, so I freed him from the warmth of my mouth, assumed the position by laying on my stomach.

"Give it to me doggystyle baby." He was on top of me in a flash and within no time, I had him screaming like a love stick little bitch. "This is some good vagina. Oh Shitt. You got it right baby. Oh shit, this is the best vagina I ever had," he screamed as he slapped my ass. He was enjoying his self so much, I had a feeling this was going to be quick, and I was right. He barely lasted five minutes, but that was okay. I'd achieved my goal. Those five minutes must have felt like an eternity to Keisha, who was bawling in my ear the whole time. After he had his orgasm, he rolled over next to me on the bed.

I said sweetly, "Do you always meet your women at this Rex, downtown?" He looked at me and gave some answer, but I wasn't really interested. It was more to enlighten Keisha's darkness.

I was listening to her say "Rex..downtown..ok.. Wait till I see you bitch." I laughed. As if she thought I would actually wait for her to get here. I had more important things on my agenda. Like putting my winnings to use right now. Wings Fiesta this Friday, so I need to get the ball rolling. I disconnected the call. I figured I had an extra thirty minutes to spear before Keisha arrived. So I opted for round two. Maybe I can get my fix this time around and he wouldn't nut so quickly.

"Are you ready for round 2 hun?" I said as I reached and massaged his shaft. He was hard in an instant and was not reluctant at all to show me just how ready he was. I hoist my ass and assumed the position once more. But just like the first time, he got his with a quickness and collapsed onto my back. Maybe my theory about muscle guys wasn't far-fetched after all. But if things were supposed to go as planned, I needed to get out of here. I nudged him off me and he stretched out on his back, his jimmy glistening limply on his thigh, I wore him and his muscle out.

"Be right back baby," I said as I scooped up my clothes and headed toward the bathroom. He didn't bother to answer, and I knew he was already on his way into post-sex slumber. By the time I tiptoed out of the bathroom, I heard light snoring, so I kept it moving to the front door.

I laughed at the thought of the stress she was about to put him through when she saw him, but he deserved it. Men should really learn the concept of loyalty and stop being so quick to cheat. They are too darn greedy. I headed towards the lobby and looked if there was any sign of Keisha but to no avail. I went on my merry way. Then it dawned on me. I think a car needs to be next on my list. This constant reliance on a taxi to get around was working my last nerve.

****

I left Rex Hotel and went straight to Ashley's Furniture store. I had my eyes on a few pieces that I needed for my business and with the help of Dean, I was now able to make my down-payment. I paid for same day delivery and was excited about setting them up tonight. I still had about ten thousand remaining, so I headed to the meat mart and picked up a few things. This wasn't really needed for tonight as I had already meal prepped from the night before.

The moment I got home, I cleaned up outside and set up my new furniture. My mother stood in the doorway watching my every move with a smile on her face before she finally approached me and told me how proud she was that business was going well. What mommy doesn't know, wouldn't hurt her, and I intended to keep things that way. I finished up outside then went into the kitchen and placed the first batch of chicken wings inside the deep fryer. This was just about my last few minutes of freedom, because everything was about to happen quickly.

Before I knew it, the place was jam packed. Vehicles were parked along other avenues because the parking lot for my court was full to capacity. Some even blocked a few of the neighbours' driveway. In all the staging of Wings Fiesta, I had never seen this turn out. I was tremendously grateful; maybe this was my breakthrough. It looked like everything was about to fall in place. I am glad that I purchased supplies earlier, because by the look of things, I would have needed extra of everything tonight. Under normal circumstance, it would be me and one other person who prepared the food along with two persons serving, but tonight even mommy was in the kitchen. That had never happened before. At one point, even Briana helped out with the serving. I was grateful for friends like her who just jumped in to help without being asked.

Things got so crazy that I totally forgot t I was supposed to meet her new boyfriend tonight. I opted to fix them a nice plate and introduced myself briefly before returning to my duties. But after realizing that her new man was white, we definitely needed a do over. By the looks of things, my girl had hit the jackpot. I am yet to hear of a white man in our country who was not earning more than the average person. Besides, rich men were known to gravitate towards Bri. She was a magnet for them. I wish I had that charm. In the brief conversation we had, he seemed like a nice person, and she seemed happy. As long as she was happy, I was ok with everything else.

I chatted briefly with Bri, in the kitchen before resuming my duties. I served a plate for the disc jock who was doing an amazing job getting patrons to have a great time on the dance floor.

This was also a first time occurrence. I took a few moments just gazing out the door at the view. It seemed surreal. This was all me. This was my business. Hundreds of persons showed up, and I was grateful. To my surprise, even Duane stopped by. He has never supported any of the other stagings. Apparently, it wasn't in line with what Christ would approve of, all because my dj played everything but gospel. I couldn't change this, because it's what the people preferred. Besides, it annoyed me that he was of that view. Is it sinful if I attended a restaurant or lounge or some event where genres of music other than gospel being played? If that's the case, then Christians should not go anywhere then. He was too ardent and ridiculous. I was annoyed. He insisted on purchasing a meal, even though I offered him a plate on the house. Maybe, he was trying to make up for our lunch date, even though it wasn't his fault I had to leave. Whatever the motive, I appreciated the business.

The mood continued all night. The patrons were festive. They ate and danced the night away until about 1 am; that's when the crowd slowly dwindled. I started the cleanup process at this point, so it wouldn't seem so burdensome the next day.

The night was hectic, so I am sure I would have slept in late the following morning. I also utilized this slow period to chat a little with Briana and Steve, who seemed cool; he was easy to talk to. I could see why she liked him. They stayed until everything ended.

Because I was still on a high from such a large crowd, that I ended up cleaning the place thoroughly at the end of the event. Mom provided some assistance. By the time I finished, it was about 4am. I locked myself in my room and totaled my sales. After deducting payment for my staff and overall cost to purchase groceries for the next staging, I still had a generous amount remaining. I took up a stash of thousand dollar bills, kissed it and screamed, "thank you Jesus!" He finally answered my prayers. I even rewarded my mother for her assistance. Tonight was the best staging of Wings Fiesta. I wished every Friday could have been like this. I texted Bri to share my excitement before retiring to bed.

17

Briana

Not sure what was happening, but I think this was the first staging of Wings Fiesta that I had ever seen with such a large turn-out. The patrons were so engaged; they were dancing, eating and having a good time. Most times people sat in their groups, chatted, ate then left. But this staging was like a party. I was so excited by the success of the event, because I knew this meant more sales which meant more money which ultimately resulted in a super happy Kim. We all knew how the lack of money made her cranky. This also meant that she probably wouldn't be able to spend much time at the table with Steve and I. Anastasia and Bugz were also present, but they stayed by themselves tonight. I found that odd but never questioned it. Melonie sat with Steve and I. Steve on the other hand, was very observant tonight. He wasn't his usual talkative self, but I supposed that was because he wasn't really familiar with Melonie. He was, however, enjoying the music and the drinks. Melonie went on to express her feelings for Alex to me. It's almost as if she was seeking my permission to date him. Of course, I am sure Steve was mentally making notes of this conversation. I knew he gathered that Alex was my ex; quite frankly, it really didn't matter to me who he dated. But then, I thought about something for a few minutes. I wondered if he was dating Melonie as an attempt to make me jealous, especially since I rejected his invite to go on a date. This was a stunt he was more than capable of. He was very petty and revengeful. So far, he had proven himself to be an expert at toying with women's emotions. My only advice to Melonie was to be vigilant, in relation to Alex. I urged her to pay attention even to the little things. Who knows, maybe he has changed, though I really doubted that. Still, I wasn't about to fill her head with negatives in an effort to poison her mind against him. Everyone is different and there is no telling how their story may unfold. I excused myself from the table and went inside to greet Kim.

She was busy sharing food. She paused and came to hug me as soon as she saw me. "I would help you but I can't leave Steve by himself."

"Oh no.. I totally forgot you were bringing him. I don't have much time on my hands tonight to chit chat with him. This turn-out is ridiculous but I am loving it."

"I bet you are. Chi Ching…," I said rubbing my fingers together."

"Girl YAAAASSSSSSSS," she said with a broad smile on her face. Let me at least fix you all a nice plate and introduce myself to him before disappearing once more."

I assisted her and we both headed back to our table. We handed each person a plate after which she asked where is Steve. "I am right here," he said in his sexy Canadian accent.

"Hello Steve" Kim said, scrutinizing him from head to toe before smiling and shaking his hand. "I have heard so much about you. It's nice to finally meet you. It's only a pity, I can't dine with you tonight, but we definitely need a do-over Mr Steve. "

"Name the time and place, and we will make it happen."

"I like you already."

We all laughed. "That means no hot oil then?" I added. Kim and I both laughed, but Steve looked confused. I returned with Kim to the house to get drinks for every one when she nudged me then said "You didn't tell me Steve was white. Where on earth did you find him?"

I laughed.

"I met him, while I was on one of my charity missions."

"Sign me up. I think I suddenly feel the spirit of volunteerism." I swear among Kim, Steve and the patients at work, my days tend to be filled with laughter. I loved my life and the people in it.

"When you decide to do that thing let me know if the old adage is true..."

"What adage is that?"

"You know...that white men have small penises?"

"Jesus Kim...Get out of here. I am not here for this." I punched her in the arm, grabbed the drinks then left.

I chatted with Steve and Melonie for a little while before she decided to leave. I waited for the right time to go over and say hi to Bugz and Anastasia, but that moment never came. They seemed to have been arguing, and they left heated.

Steve and I were the last ones standing. We danced and chatted and had a great time. We ended up staying until everyone left at about 2am. That was the time Kim joined us at the table. To my surprise, they were both full of energy and a conversation ensued. They eventually got a chance to get familiar with each other. We stayed for an additional hour after which we left. Thank God I wasn't working tomorrow, because I was tired.

While journeying home, Steve mentioned that he had a proposition for me.

"I have to leave for Miami next Friday for the weekend to work on a project. I would like you to accompany me, and I promise you will have a great time. We could do a movie or party in south beach the Friday night; we would stay at a terrific hotel, go swimming, shopping or whatever you wanted on the Saturday plus a few dinner dates in the mix then come home on Sunday. Would you like to go with me? He looked hopeful as he asked me?"

"Will this be a room with a single or double bed?"

He laughed at my question.

"That's up to you sweetie. Whatever your choice, the offer still stands."

We had been out quite a few times, and I think it was safe to say that we were crazy about each other, so why not spend the weekend with him. I had a private moment thinking about his offer but then my thoughts were rudely interrupted by Kim's voice also in my subconscious calling me a vestal virgin. I laughed out loud before giving him an answer.

"Yes, I would like that. I think a King bed would be perfect as well."

"I think so too. He took my hands and kissed it. It's going to be fun."

"I don't doubt that," I responded, beaming at him.

18

Kim

I needed good old fashioned retail therapy; and if there was one thing I knew how to do, it's to shop. Now that I was able to buy without a budget, it just made things all the more exciting. All my life I have been jumping from dick to dick just to pay the bills and pamper myself, though it was mainly the latter; I had finally gotten my heart's desire. Since juggling Dean, Duane and Hugh, I was able to live comfortably. Hugh contributed significantly to my comfort; with him I hit the jackpot. I was finally able to buy all the brand name clothing, get my Brazilian hair installed on a regular basis, manicure, pedicure , facial, massages-just about everything I needed, whenever I desired. I was living my 'Pretty Woman' moment, and I was loving it.

Still, things were a bit complicated, because Hugh wanted me to put an end to Wings Fiesta. I had mixed feelings about this because I had benefitted a great deal from this business. Furthermore, this was my passion, and I was motivated especially by the success of the last two stagings. Even though there were days when I regret that I ever started the business, I was pleased by how much it had grown. Now, I was torn between giving up what I had worked so hard to build and now being offered everything I had ever financially longed on a platter. I was unable to think logically about the situation when everything dangled before me. I had my own fully furnished apartment in an upscale community and a brand-new Mercedes. There was no way I would be able to keep my chicken business thriving in such environs; now that I had basically moved out, my mother would not approve of-me keeping the event at her house. She was also angry at me because she noticed that I had strayed from the house of the Lord. She also had no interest in coming to view my new apartment. She claimed it was either obtained from blood money or some form of illegal activity that she didn't want to be associated with. Though I still had not uttered a word concerning our relationship status, I accepted the benefits and even stayed in the apartment three to four nights weekly. I really didn't know what to do. Technically, I didn't need Wings Fiesta because Hugh had enough money to maintain his wife and I. Though the sense of independence was a beautiful feeling, I think I may take my chances and attempt to enjoy the best of both worlds. I will figure something out. For now, my focus was on my car; this Mercedes gave me life. I was eager to show Briana, so I called her.

"Hey sweetie, what's up?"

"Nothing much Hun, I am here enjoying the weekly drama in my community"

"Sounds like a pretty chill day on your end. Does that mean you will be home the whole day then?"

"Yes as far as I know. Unless you are coming to get me so we can go out? If you are not, please bring me a bottle of wine. My stash is dry."

"No problem, see you soon." I dressed myself in one of my cute shorts outfit then headed to Briana's house.

By the time I pulled up in her driveway in my new Mercedes, I was bursting with happiness. Driving a top of the line German vehicle will lift your mood anytime. Briana was already outside in the garden. I watched her squint her eyes as she tried to make out the person behind the steering wheel who parked in her drive way. I rolled my windows down before yelling "It's me Heifer" with a smile planted on my face.

Her jaws dropped. She ran towards the vehicle with pure excitement and jumped in the passenger seat. "Oh my God Kimberly. A 2017 Mercedes Benz CLS; look at this interior." I don't know what the hell Bri was talking about but it all sounded so sexy as it rolled off her tongue. "Kim what the hell is going on?"

"Girl this is my new ride."

"You must have done monkey flips on that D or fried his chicken in diamond oil for this to be handed down to you. I need to take a leave out of your book because...."

I laughed uncontrollably.

"You know I like nice things," was all I managed to say.

"Like nice things is an understatement. You hit the freaking jackpot. This Benz is giving me all sorts of feels right now."

"Tell me about it. I have been feeling like a million dollars."

"You know I think this would go perfectly with my outfit tomorrow," Bri added.

"What outfit? You wear scrubs to work; girl bye."

"I hope you brought that wine because you have some explaining to do."

"Yes mommy" I responded as we both exited the vehicle and went inside the house.

The minute the door closed the interrogation begun.

"So who's Mercedes are you sporting?"

"It's mine."

"Under what conditions?" she asked as she opened the wine and poured two glasses.

"There are no conditions." Bri paused and shot me a deadly look.

"Nothing you said just now made sense. You do realize you are driving a high-end vehicle?"

I took a sip of the wine. "I don't know. I haven't thought about it just yet. It's still so complicated."

"The fact that the keys of the Benz are in your possession, you must have given an answer?"

"No I haven't, though I partially moved in but…"

"What? Move in where?" she interrupted.

"He gave me a fully furnished apartment in addition to the car with a proposal for me to be his mistress. Of course, I am to offer myself to only him and apparently I need to put an end to Wings Fiesta."

The look on Briana's face told me that I had a lecture coming.

"Where would I keep the event? You know if I move out mom will tell me to host my event elsewhere since I no longer lived there. You know how difficult she can be."

"I agree with mommy. If you are on your own, then you need to manage your responsibilities accordingly. How about you get a place to rent or consider purchasing a property. Maybe even diversify the event from just Wings on Fridays. Maybe you can have other themed nights, like crayfish Thursdays, soup Saturdays, pasta Tuesdays etc. This could be your way to finally establish yourself in an industry you love. Besides, your man has the capital to help you start so why not capitalize on that? I don't see why you are thinking of putting an end to it. This thing has been your bread and butter; yet you are willing to toss it away in the wink of an eye, because a man tells you to? Who is he by the way?"

"Hugh Brenton," I told her nonchalantly.

It took her a second then her eyes got big and she shouted. "Hugh Brenton, as in the CEO of…"

"Yup that would be him," I said interrupting her.

"Shit. You hit the lottery for sure."

"I tell you all the time that I am allergic to poverty. My aim in this life is to never be broke."

"Well if you keep jumping into situations like this without any fruitful long term plan, you are bound to hit rock bottom; and when you do, there may be no coming back."

Briana's words hurt really badly, because I knew what she said was absolutely true. I wasn't as level-headed as her so I didn't plan things out as carefully as she did. I guess that is one of the key things successful people did.

"Though I am not really liking the package he presented, that you seem to have accepted, I can't tell you what to do. But all I know is that you need to think about this carefully. The man is married…"

"Who are you to judge me?" I interrupted her.

"Please let me finish Kim. I am not judging you. Furthermore, I have an advantage of throwing stones at you for dating a married man. Yes, I am guilty of that as well but the difference is…you are a Christian. You are supposed to uphold and honour these things more than anyone else. You are the one living a double standard life. Kim, I am not trying to argue with you. I care about

188

you, and I just don't want to see you make the same mistakes twice. You hit rock bottom once before and you did an amazing job to pick yourself up. I just don't want to see you give that all up because the grass seems greener on Hugh's side at the moment." She paused for a moment and looked at me as if trying to get me to see things her way.

"I know you like material things," she continued, "but all I am saying is that you need to consider using him to establish yourself in a more long term manner. As I was saying before you rudely interrupted me, he is married. And I know that man has no intentions of leaving his wife for you. Secondly, you were given a vehicle plus apartment and the title of his mistress. Not only are you his mistress, but I am sure he will demand to know your whereabouts and as you said, he wants you to give up Wings Fiesta. Let me bring it all home for you. You will be expected to be his woman on the side and be available whenever he needs you. That means you are obligated to solely him. So, erase the thought of dating other men and the possibilities of marriage and family if that was ever on the agenda. He will control your every move, because you are now his investment. You have no job or anything to look forward to because you are his prized trophy. You will forever be dependent on him.

I remained quiet. I let her speak, because she was my friend, and we have been through a lot together; plus, I knew she meant well; plus, she was making some valid points.

She paused again, briefly, looked hard at me and continued her lecture.

"Let's say for whatever reason, things go sour. What do you have to support yourself or who do you turn to? Are you comfortable running back to mommy every time life throws you lemons? If you truly understand what you are getting into accepting that Benz then go right ahead and do your thing. I am not saying you can't indulge. Sex becomes a business at some point in time for some of us. There is no shame in the game, but be smart and very careful about it. Especially since these men today are killing women for little or nothing. Whatever you decide to do, just don't give up Wings Fiesta. Those honey glazed chicken wings are to die for."

I laughed at her last remark. But for the most part, I felt like I just wanted to curl up in a ball after listening to Briana. Everything she said was the truth, but I don't know, this Benz was everything. I needed more time to think about it.

"Anyway, how is the sex?" she asked. Thank God she changed the subject because I was becoming edgy.

"Nothing mind-blowing but you know I will fake orgasms if I have to in order to stay in possession of my lottery ticket." We laughed in unison. We ended up spending the rest of the afternoon watching a movie and almost finishing two bottles of wine.

****

A call from Duane interrupted the beautiful moment I was sharing with my bestie. Before I could even answer, I was greeted by the words "we need to talk Kim". He later added that he would stop by my home shortly. I told him I was at Briana's place, but he demanded that I returned home to meet with him. He sounded angry. I don't think I had ever seen or heard him that worked up before. I hugged Bri then left. I felt slightly woozy, but I was able to drive home safely. I parked my car at my neighbour's house in attempt to hide it from Duane. Last thing I needed was another person breathing down my neck about my decisions. I hurried inside, and he arrived about 5 minutes later. I opened the grill for him, and during the time we both exchanged stares. I led him to my bedroom and still he remained silent. When a man wants to talk, it's always a good idea to let him do the talking. If he wouldn't start the conversation then neither would I. He pressed up in my face real close like he was about to kiss me but he asked one question.

"Kim what are you doing? I am tired of playing games. You hardly talk to me. You make no effort for us to spend quality time together as we usually do. What is really going on with you? Do you want to end this, because I feel like I am wasting my time here? So tell me what is going on Kim? Am I wasting my time?" He hardly paused to take a breath.

Too many questions to answer all at once, I thought to myself. I was cornered and wasn't sure how to answer without hurting him. It's not that I wasn't attracted to him. He was a sweetheart, but lately I had been preoccupied with Hugh and Dean. Duane was broke like myself. He was just an ordinary young man looking to make something of himself. He was very ambitious, and he was serious about church. All this time we had been together, he never touched me. I sometimes wondered if he ever felt horny, because he had never made remarks about anything sexual, neither to me nor around me. This bugged me a lot. To make matters worse, he seemed like he was well endowed in that department and there was no way to find out. If I am to be honest with myself, I would say that Duane is a good man, and I think I could grow to love him. He was husband material. But I loved money-something he did not have. So now I was faced with the issue of money vs love. My mind drifted to the lecture with Briana earlier as she presented the option of ambition and long term goals as opposed to just being able to leisurely obtain money. I wished everyone would leave me alone.

"I would like an answer today Kim?" Duane demanded. His voice drew me back to the present. I didn't know what to say. I didn't want to hurt his feelings.

"I don't know Duane. You are a nice guy, but I don't know if I can make this relationship work."

"Why is that?" he asked. I wish I knew the answer.

"I don't know. I had a rough life. I know how to hustle. I don't know how to love a man the right way or what it means to really be loved."

"Then let me show you. Stop shutting me out and allow us to experience the concept together."

"I can't...I am sorry Duane, but I really can't." A text message came in on my cell phone, and I glanced at it. It was Hugh telling me he was on his way to the apartment. I responded to his text then he responded with an answer that irked. He basically ordered me to be present at the apartment before he got there. Not sure what his problem was.

"Can you give the phone a break, so we can have a serious conversation for once Kim? You rushed off the last time we were supposed to have lunch together and you are yet to schedule time to make it up to me. Instead, you have become distant. Is there someone else?"

An awkward pregnant pause followed his question. He took that to mean consent.

"I figured as much. I just needed to hear you say it to my face. I treated you like a queen, so I expect that this person must be treating you way better than I did."

After hearing this, I held my head down shamefully. I had hurt him, but I wasn't sure I wanted to mend it. I need money. That is what makes me happy. Why can't I have a man who is rich, great in bed and good looking? Was that too much to ask for?

"I can accept you turning your back on me. That's life. You win some, and you lose some but don't turn your back on God. You have gotten too far to toss it all away so easily. Please don't stop fighting or praying, promise me that. That's all I ask of you. It was really nice to have met you Kim." Those were his last words. He kissed me on my forehead then left.

I don't know why I felt like I just lost a very important piece to this puzzle called life, but still I did nothing to stop him. Although it hurt, I felt it was best to let him go. Now, I had to prepare myself to face Hugh's drama. I was still somewhat woozy and would love to relax in bed but I knew I wouldn't hear the end of it from

Hugh. I grabbed my keys and made my way to the apartment. Everyone wore me out today.

Hugh was clearly anxiously awaiting my arrival because the minute I walked through the door he attacked me. He grabbed me angrily by my arm before saying "You try'na play me?"

"Whu…what?" I stuttered in astonishment.

"I told you I was at home."

"Why do you need to be home when you have a place here? I told you to pack your stuff and move them in."

"You told me? I never told you that I accepted your proposal. I need time to think about it."

"You need time to think about my proposal, yet you are parading in my Benz?"

I couldn't believe he just said that. Did Hugh think that giving me his Benz was his free ticket to owning me? There was no way that was going to happen. Worst he was sloppy in bed. It's going to take more than his money to keep me rooted. But I wasn't ready to give him up just yet. I hadn't even started reaping my benefits. I leaned over and kissed him on the mouth, deep, wet and prying. I needed it all to stop. First Briana, then Duane now Hugh. I had too much interrogation for one day. I felt a headache coming on.

Hopefully sex will calm him down and buy me a few more days. He opened himself up to me and pressed his pelvis against mine. He buried his face in my neck before whispering "you are mine."

Looks like Briana was right. It has begun already. How the hell was I going to pull this off? Before I could start to worry, Hugh picked me up and carried me to the bedroom.

I sold my soul to the devil.

****

I was more than stressed from all that was happening than I was willing to admit to anyone and to myself. Life was coming at me fast. Having moved out of my mother's house for a second time and having to put my business on hold for a while had all taken a toll on me. Hugh's constant fussing about my whereabouts or simply not being available to meet his demands whenever he desired, slowly sucked all the energy out of me. I felt like a little puppet who was trying to make everyone happy. Having the best of both worlds was harder than I thought.

I met with Dean for lunch as a means of taking my mind off all the drama. I had not hooked up with him since my payback to his annoying girlfriend. He was still chasing me though, and I was not surprised. Any man I laid this kitty on was bound to be hooked. One more time for the road wouldn't hurt, at least that's what I told myself. I really didn't care about Dean. This little rendezvous was just a means to an end, so I wouldn't have to be so dependent on Hugh. This little rendezvous was a necessity, because my only source of income, other than my reliance on Hugh, was now my lunch prep duties for the school, which Hugh was still unhappy about.

I figured that sleeping with other men and fleecing money may help my relationship with Hugh in the long run. That way I wouldn't have to resent the fact that Hugh had too much control over my life, and I wouldn't be too dependent on him financially; that way, I would not have had any reason to want to leave him. At least, that's how I tried to reason out the situation. I picked up the cherry from my drink and sucked it between my lips. I was so lost in thought, I was totally oblivious to the fact that Dean was sitting across the table from me, until he held my hands and placed them on his muscular thighs. I was suddenly reminded of how much of a wimp Hugh was with his soggy legs and flabby belly. Dean had a perfectly chiseled body. He was just a reminder of the sexy men I had given up just to be with Hugh.

"Do you think we can re-do that moment only this time without the drama?" He asked, as he continued to guide my hands along his thighs.

"Once you provide me with pocket money, sure; I am all yours."

He smiled. "You know I got you hun."

I immediately thought about that Gucci purse and shoes I had seen. I could pair them with the fitted jeans I had purchased a week ago. I tried to calculate how much time I would need to travel to his place, get him off and make it back in time to catch that store before they closed. I told him that I was extremely horny as an excuse for him to cut our lunch date short. As he drove to his place, I massaged his crotch the whole time as I thought about the money I was about to receive. Then I got a bright idea to initiate a blow job as he drove home that way he would have been overly excited by the time we got to the apartment, and I would get him off in a minute. My idea worked. He couldn't wait to devour me.

He literally ripped off his clothes before closing the door behind him. I pulled off my top and allowed my breasts to spill out like wild children. This drove him crazy. He buried his face between them and made this roaring sound. This I found amusing. "Easy there boy," I said patting his head as he dug in and shifted from nipple to nipple. It wasn't long before he hoisted my skirt, bent me over and thrust in me powerfully. This was way better than the first time, and he was also going much longer- way longer than I had anticipated; this was messing up my agenda. So I switched to a different plan. I shoved him on the bed and assumed my cowgirl mode. I snuggled myself on top of him and rode him fiercely.

The more I rode, the louder I screamed. Between the noise and the speed, I could tell that he was about to nut. He begged for me to slow down and even held on to my waist in an attempt to control the movement, but my speed overpowered him. Before I knew it, he was screaming like a girl. Finally, I said in my thoughts. I think I had about one hour to spare until closing time.

I hopped off him and rushed to the bathroom to freshen up. But then in a brief moment I looked at my reflection in the mirror and felt some form of remorse. I didn't quite understand what was happening. This had never before happened to me post sex. I looked at the person in the mirror and saw a woman who had slept with another woman's man, not once but twice. "Stop it!!" I spoke to myself in the mirror. "You need to get it together."

"Are you ok in there?" I supposed he heard the mumbling. "Yes dear, I am fine." I shook my shoulders then proceeded to dress myself. By the time I came out of the restroom, I went straight for the wallet that had fallen out of his pocket when he hastily undressed.

"Damn girl, you don't waste no time." He said sitting up in the bed with his sexy fully naked body.

"I have errands to run. Call me if anything." I blew him kisses then left. If I had the car, I would have made it to the store with adequate time to spare but I opted to travel via public transportation for a little while until Hugh calmed down. He was making too many references to his Mercedes, as if it was God's best gift to man.

Peak hour traffic was not as terrible as I had imagined, so I arrived at approximately 15 minutes before closing time. This was good enough for me as I knew exactly what I wanted and where to find them. At 5pm, I was strolling out the store with my head high and my Gucci apparels in hand.

19

Briana

The following work week went by quickly. I ended up taking the weekend off, something that I hadn't done in a while. I took an additional day off during the week in order to get my hair and nails done. This trip with Steve was like a mini honey moon to me. It's been awhile since I have had an actual getaway with someone. It was hard to have moments like these with Chris, because he was married.

Steve handled all the flight and hotel arrangements. Even though I offered to pay a portion, he felt insulted by the fact that I even suggested that. He purchased tickets for us to travel in first class and we both watched a movie and slept until we landed. He dropped me off at the hotel then left for work. I didn't mind soaking up the ambience on my own. Besides, I lived alone for most of my life, so I have mastered enjoying my own company. We stayed at Mandarin Oriental in Miami; a very luxurious and elegant hotel. We stayed in one of the suites that offered a dramatic view of the bay and Miami's skyline. The place was very impressive thus far; excellent choice by Steve. I toured the hotel grounds and made my way to the spa. This was also long overdue. I settled on a full body deep tissue massage and a refresher facial. By the time I completed treatment, I was starved. I returned to my suite and requested room service. I had one weekend to live it up, and I was doing just that. While devouring my meal, the phone rang. It was Steve checking up on me. It was clear that he felt guilty leaving me alone, but I reassured him that I was ok. He wasn't convinced until I told him how I had been spending the day. He told me he would have been home by 7 that night and that he had made dinner reservations for 9. After ending the call with him, I fell asleep.

When I woke up it was 7 exactly. Steve still wasn't home as yet; but I showered and got dressed nevertheless. It usually takes me forever to get ready, so I ensured that I would not have kept him waiting....at least not for long. I was wearing a red, body fitting dress that was elegant but short enough to show off my legs. I don't think I had ever dressed so sexily in his presence before. I hoped he liked it. He got in shortly after eight, immediately rushing off to take a shower and dressed himself while I tuned in to Real Housewives.

He showered, shaved and got dressed in about twenty minutes which was record time to me. I could have never gotten ready in such short time. When he came out the room looking unbelievably sexy in his navy blue suit and white shirt, it sparked the same reaction it did the first time I saw him at the children's home.

"You look fabulous!!" I exclaimed. "And you my darling, look ravishing," he responded.

Hand in hand, we headed out to the Brasserie restaurant which was across the road from the hotel we stayed. It was an Italian restaurant.

"We look very cute together," I said as we sat at our table in Brasserie.

"I agree. I am proud to be by your side," he responded. "So how did the project go?"

"Quite productive," he began and told me all about it. I was impressed by the fact that he was so passionate about what he did, and by all appearances, he did his job very well. He must be great at his job if he gets privileges to travel across the globe and gets a heavy discount at the various hotels. I don't think regular employees were treated with such royalty. I think our relationship to date, thrived on mutual respect and admiration for each other. We both enjoyed our meals.

We walked along the strip and spotted a little club that we stayed for about 2 hours. We drank some more, and it was the first time I had really seen Steve truly unwinding. He was always the automatic designated driver whenever we went out, so he was never really able to drink much. But this weekend was different for him. I saw him in all his elements. He was not as bad of a dancer as I thought he would have been either. The way he danced tonight, was totally different from the way he danced at Wings Fiesta, maybe it was the alcohol? I don't know what it was, but I loved it. I was enjoying every second in his presence. We had a blast at the club. We laughed and talked as we made our way back to the hotel but the moment I walked into the suite, it suddenly hit me that I was spending the night with a man. I supposed he sensed the panic in me.

"Briana...it's going to be ok. We don't have to do anything you are not comfortable with. I could even sleep on the couch, if that makes you comfortable?" he said as he kissed me.

Why was he tripping? Which man is going to spend a weekend with a woman in another country and not want to rip her clothes off? As much as this was a minor concern for me, I appreciated the fact that he tried to be understanding and wasn't forceful by any means. We laid in each other's arms in the suite's living room couch and peered out the window. A very romantic and breathtaking view. We cuddled, kissed, caressed, until he eventually unzipped my dress. He unbuttoned my bra while I unbuttoned his shirt and before long, we were both butt naked. I was pleasantly surprised by his athletic body. I didn't expect him to look like that at his age but I guess his busy lifestyle and occasional work out routines at home kept him in shape. I ran my hands over his body and suddenly didn't feel shy anymore. His desire for me was plainly obvious, and

I was completely turned on by that; so, moments later we made love right there on the couch. It was perfect just like everything else between us so far. We came together; afterward, he laid on top of me panting and out of breath. He eased off, reached for my hands and led me to the bedroom. We huddled beside each other on the bed.

"Mercy!!! Then you claim you are shy. You are bound to give me a heart attack", he said. I laughed and then we fooled around with each other, until we wound up making love again; it was even better than before.

"Listen Briana. I don't care what you want to say, but you are officially my woman. I am never going to let you get out of bed. Maybe we should retire." I laughed. He was so silly. We talked and joked around until we finally fell asleep with him cuddled up behind me.

In the morning, I was up before he was. I watched him sleep comfortably. He looked so peaceful and sexy. It's safe to say that Steve was officially mine; he was my man. Pleased with what I saw, I was instantly overwhelmed with desire, so I woke him up. He made love to me again, then we went back to sleep for another hour. The next time we both woke up, I showered and prepped to go shopping; meanwhile, he ordered room service.

I came out of the bathroom in my robe and bed slippers.

"You are so beautiful," he said as he leaned over to kiss me. He could hardly keep his hands off me, and I could see and feel his excitement once more. I gave in to his desire once again before he rushed to shower and dressed himself. We ate, then headed out to the mall.

Steve shopped with me for the first half hour, but then he left me with a wad of cash and told me to meet him by the internet café when I was done. He had to do a conference call for work. When I flipped through the stash, I initially thought this was too much money but after visiting a few branded outlets, it was almost finished. I had to stop at Victoria's Secret and Bath & Body Works with what I had left. There was no way a shopping adventure is complete without fragrances. I would probably have to use my own money to pick up something for Kim. Either way, I was content. I met up with Steve in the food court with Lord knows how many shopping bags. He shook his head, when I approached him and exclaimed that he was glad he didn't come with me. We had lunch at Ihop before returning to the hotel where we spent the rest of the day by the poolside. Steve seemed to enjoy this more than I did. After a few drinks and basking in the pelting sun. We were both drained. We went back to the room, dozed off and woke up just in time to dress for dinner.

This time I stunned him with a dress that was even shorter than the one last night; this was deliberately paired with some stiletto heels; I could tell he was even more impressed.

"Sweetheart, why don't you dress as sexily back home?"

I laughed. That was a good question.

"I am not sure. There was something about vacations. I always feel relaxed and carefree. I guess at home, you are known by people so you try to maintain a certain reputation or simply just to look appropriate at all times."

"If you care so much about what people think about your appearance now, then can you imagine if you were popular? You would be on some Kim Kardashian mentality."

I laughed out loud.

"Well, it looks like I will have to take you on vacations across the globe more often then."

"Sounds about right," winking at him. This time we dined at Truluck's restaurant. The ambience was amazing. The live band in the background while we dined was also very nice. We had a lighthearted conversation over yet another fabulous meal before returning to the hotel, where we made love. We both watched the movie Fifty Shades of Grey, stopping occasionally to kiss and cuddle until we made love again and finally fell asleep.

We had breakfast the next morning then headed to this place that allowed you to participate in exotic car racing. This was one of the best low key things to do in Miami. I usually get a rush from driving go karts but this blew my mind. I got a chance to drive a Lamborghini Huracan while Steve drove a Ferrari GT. I was given the opportunity to drive one of my dream cars on a real speed track. Needless to say I did put the gas pedal to use. My adrenaline was pumping the whole time. It was the most exhilarating thing I had ever done; a one of a kind experience. As soon as it ended, I was on a high on our way back to the hotel. We packed our bags, then headed to the airport an hour later to fly home.

I slept the entire journey back with my head on his shoulders. I was relaxed and totally at ease with him. It had been the best weekend of my life and before he headed in the direction of my home, he asked me to stay with him.

"Are you sure? You are not tired of me yet after such a long weekend?" I asked.

"I am falling in love with you, "he responded. It was so welcoming to hear those words. Someone loving me and solely me. I tried hard not to blush at what he said. He showed me where everything was and I interrupted the tour by diving into his bed. "Now, there is a gorgeous sight." He said as he bent over and kissed me. Afterwards, I swam naked in his pool and he watched me. We discussed the news, stock market trends and what it meant for the economy.

Following that, I dried myself and went back into the house where we slept soundly until my alarm went off at 6 am for me to get ready for work. That little shopping spree came in handy because I had to pull from my stash of new clothing to head to work. I smiled broadly when he opened the room door carrying a tray.

"Chef Steve," I teased as he approached me. He prepared me a meal of Spanish omelet, French toast, and a bowl of fruits with a cup of coffee. You can't do me wrong with a cup of coffee. It was my daily fix.

He looked at me pensively, "I don't want to creep you out, but I think I do love you," he said as he leaned over to kiss me.

This weekend taught me a lot about him, and I wasn't putting a time span to it. I was living in the moment. I was happy with Steve. "I love you too," I responded. An hour later we both got dressed and left for work.

****

Fresh off a mini vacay, I was having a superb day at work. I couldn't help but reminisce on the most amazing weekend with Steve. I was well sexed and relaxed. Today, I was scheduled for rounds on the labour ward. I have delivered hundreds of babies since I have been in midwifery, but it never gets old. On the labour ward, you get to see people from all walks of life, and you are exposed to people at their most emotional and vulnerable time. Every baby's birth is special. Every delivery makes me teary-eyed because I am still amazed by the miracle of birth; not to mention the strength and courage of women. But some births were simply unforgettable.

The birth that started my morning was also one of a lifetime. I delivered quadruplets. I had never done that before so being the midwife on duty for this mother was a real privilege. The moment the one girl followed by three boys came out crying in good condition, tears streamed down my face. I congratulated their incredible mom and watched as she shared the sheer delight with her husband that all her babies were healthy.

A few minutes later, I checked on another patient of mine, with whom I had developed a great rapport. She was 8cm dilated and almost ready, so I updated her husband. The man behaved very strangely. He didn't even acknowledge me when I addressed him. His gaze was fixed on the floor, clear indication that he was deliberately avoiding eye contact. Utterly annoyed by his childish behavior, I decided to say something.

"You know you can at least pretend to care about the information I am providing you about your wife? Why are you even here if you are going to act this way?

You are making things harder for her with this attitude. She doesn't need any additional stress." I said angrily.

"I want to be here. I wouldn't miss this moment," he said as he finally looked up at me.

"Then start acting like it," was the last thing I said before walking off, but then I stopped in my tracks.

"By the way, do I know you? You look very familiar." I asked.

"No you don't," he said sounding a bit nervous. Then he started acting creepy again with his head hanging down and eyes fixed on the floor.

I swear sometimes some people worked on my nerves. I shook my head then went on my merry way when the dots finally connected. I knew the face indeed. He had been here three weeks ago when his girlfriend had a baby. Now he is here with his wife; who I was certain had no clue. That bastard. No wonder he was acting strange. He was probably worried that I would have spilled the beans. I looked back at him and shook my head in great disbelief. UGH!!! MEN!! You can't live with them and you can't live without them.

I went back to the room to check up on the gorgeous quadruplets, and they immediately brought me back to my happy place. Shortly after, I returned to the triage room and went through my standard procedure with the newly arriving laboring women. My duties lasted until about 3pm, after which I took a one hour lunch break. I later resumed my duties; activities on the ward were slow, which I was thankful for, especially because the morning was completely hectic.

I called Kim and filled her in with the details of my trip taking care to dodge her question about the size of his penis. That, she doesn't ever need to know, but she was so persistent. I eventually distracted her by telling her that I brought a bag of goodies for her. She seemed to approve of Steve though her interaction with him was brief, but I suppose that was a good sign.

****

The bond between Steve and I developed over the next several months. We have had many disagreements and heated moments, but we always managed to work things out. It's almost been a year, and we were still going strong. I had the hots for only him. He still travelled frequently, but it seems that distance made the heart grow fonder because I yearned for him more than ever whenever he returned. I managed to travel with him occasionally as well. I also travelled to Canada and met both of his parents whom I found to be interesting. I had a good rapport with his daughter and his mother but the jury was still out on his father. He had a tendency to make racially prejudicial remarks in almost every other sentence, which clearly meant that he disapproved of his son dating a dark-skinned woman. Only time will tell how he truly feels. His daughter was very smart, ambitious and had all of Steve's physical features. Though I wasn't quite fond of his father, I was still grateful that I got a chance to meet his family.

Whenever Steve was in Jamaica, I would stay at his house but returned home as soon as he flew out. I didn't mind being in my own comfort zone. Having my own home was sometimes my saving grace from the disagreements we had. I would sleep at my place at times dependent on how heated the arguments were.

Notwithstanding, I can honestly say that I have grown a great deal being with Steve. Our relationship has forced me to tap into the duties of becoming a wife. Living on my own and cooking for my-self was totally different from having to do it to impress someone else. I now had to endure the harsh criticisms on days when the meal didn't quite turn out as I planned. Additionally, I now had to factor in what my partner craved. It was no longer just about me. Sometimes I even had to make sacrifices just to make him happy. There were days when I came home and really didn't want to do anything but to enjoy the warmth of my bed but he either needed a snack or some tender loving and care. Even though he could also manage himself in the kitchen, there were days when he felt as lazy as I did and begged for me to do it. Sometimes we did take out if neither of us felt like cooking. We had balance and I tried my best to maintain that quality. He was a powerful and a financially stable individual, and I had to constantly remind myself at moments when I couldn't be bothered with the concept of being in a relationship, that I was also benefitting from the fruits of his labour. It got hard sometimes, but I prayed consistently and asked that God helped us to work through our issues. Though I never went back to church since Kim's baptism, I never stopped praying. God has blessed me abundantly and has been too good to me for me not to give Him thanks.

Another plus about our relationship, was the depth of knowledge I acquired from him due to our age difference, and this I appreciated greatly. He was always willing to teach me new things. But there were also times when I felt insecure about my youthfulness, especially if I was in the presence of people his age group or attended formal events with him. Sometimes, I felt badly that I wasn't able to contribute to the various conversations, but this didn't bother him. He always made sure I was fixed by his side or sometimes his hands wandered to the small of my back or my ass. Whatever it may be, he always reassured me that everything would be ok. Steve became my person; I loved him.

Who would have thought I would ever say that about a man and mean it? After a slew of ill-fated relationships, I was ready to give up. At one point, I felt like I was destined to be single and grow old with cats. I am no relationship expert, but I have realized that sometimes all we needed to do was to learn the art of letting go. We need to live our lives, regardless of whether or not we were in a relationship. I learnt that we will undoubtedly screw up at times, but it's okay to live your life for you. We shouldn't wait on other persons to make moves. Relationships naturally ebb and flow over time and if it doesn't work it's still an experience to learn from. Trust that if it's to be, it will be.

20

Kim

I had gone to one of my favourite drink spots hoping to ease my mind off the world that seemed to be crumbling on my shoulders. Duane officially distanced himself from me. Initially he used to at least talk to me about church; now, he cut me off completely. He ignored all my phone calls as well. Then Bugz recently informed me that Budu had been cleared to appeal his conviction. Just the thought of Budu being out of prison resulted in me having diarrhea. I cannot imagine Budu allowing me to live a peaceful life. If he didn't torture me, death was the next alternative. I felt like no matter how I tried to run from my past, it always seemed to catch up to me. It seemed impossible to be rid of my dirty ways. Then to top it all off, I was having the worst Herpes flare since my diagnosis. The itching drove me crazy. Bathing in lightly salted water didn't seem to relieve the symptoms anymore. I had to walk around with ice packs in my underwear and ended up wearing loose clothing in order to ward off the stares of the perverts in the streets who had a thing for discussing the size of a woman's vagina. Problems backed me up in every corner.

To top things off, Hugh's attitude only worsened. I was supposed to be his puppet. But I felt angry at myself because I didn't take the foolish advice of the people who loved and cared for me. I was beginning to second-guess my lifelong mantra: *It's not about the romance, it's all about the finance.* I don't know what it was about money that got my juices flowing. There was no way I could have passed up a billion dollar lifestyle. But now that I had the world, I still wasn't happy. I needed to make a move; I needed a new game plan, but nothing came to mind. One thing I was certain of was that I no longer desired Hugh.

After three drinks and a few hours later, I arrived at the apartment tired wanting to be left alone. The moment I placed my key in the lock, the door swung open and I came face to face with Hugh. I scoffed at his presence and side-stepped him. I was utterly annoyed by his petty behavior.

"I called you several times, and you ignored my calls. I have been at the apartment since 12 and you weren't here. Where the hell have you been all this time?" he barked at me, checking me out from head to toe as if my appearance would give him some clue to the question.

"I have been out," I sashayed my sexiness past him and into the bedroom.

"What you mean by you have been out."

"Why is that so hard to understand?" I said looking him dead in the eyes. He had already worked my damn nerves.

"Who do you think you are talking to?" I heard the sound before I felt the pain, his hands crashing against my jawbone. This slap hit a nerve. My body immediately transformed into a super Saiyan mode. I shoved him so hard, he fell and slid across the room with his back crashing against the wall.

"I am not the kind of woman who likes to answer to anybody. You think your Benz and money grant you ownership of me Hugh? I had a life before you met me.

"You think I provide all of this so you can saunter your ass in here whenever you desired?" He had the nerve to do some hand sweeping motion like I was too stupid to get his point. "All of this is mine. I created this. My furniture, my Benz, my money; my world. You have no privileges here. You have no opinion about anything in this house or any right to question anything I tell you to do, not after I invest my hard-earned money in you."

His words hurt as much as the slap did. The worst part about it was that he spoke nothing but the truth. For the first time in my history of sexual escapades, I felt like a cheap little whore.

"Do you know how many women throw themselves at me to obtain what you have? Do you know how many young girls are offering sex to me just so they could get some form of cash or kind in return? I could have plucked anyone out of Lord knows how many of them, but I chose you and this is the payback I get. You ungrateful little…."

I didn't allow him to finish his sentence. "Then maybe you should go ahead and hand-pick one of those other girls who will worship you and beckon at your requests and stop stressing me?" I challenged. The shift in his demeanor was a clear indication that he was not use to confrontation.

"You think you can treat me like a punk ass little boy, who you can push around and disrespect?"

"No one said you were a punk but you sure act like one sometimes when you question my every move. Only little boys are insecure about a woman's whereabouts or don't want her to hang out with her friends. Only little boys don't want their partner to have a life of her own especially considering the fact that you are married." I continued my tirade and made my sentiments perfectly clear.

"You think owning a Mercedes, having a plush apartment in an upscale community plus access to unlimited funds and a credit card is something little boys do Kim? Do you think little boys just casually gives this to girls?"

I looked around my palace and realized that having all this luxury still did not make me happy. I am not sure what was happening to me, but it was not just about the almighty dollar anymore. The past few weeks,

I missed the peace and quiet at my mother's house. I missed organizing Wings Fiesta. I missed actually having to work and earn my money. I missed Duane and how he fussed about me, how he checked in on me daily or how he made me laugh. He didn't have funds like Hugh did, but he took care of me like a real man should. Now that is what happiness truly is. I couldn't even believe I was thinking like this.

"You need to calm down and start appreciating all that is around you. You are privileged to have all this. This is every girl's dream Kimberly. So stop clowning and get yourself together. This is as good as it gets."

"This is not happiness. I don't want it." I couldn't believe the words that flew from my mouth.

He laughed at me. "You are a money hungry, materialistic woman and you expect me to believe that this life I have created for you is not enough? This life…." He paused and made the sweeping motion once more before continuing. "This life right here….is not happiness?" he laughed even harder this time around.

"Yes. That's what I said. I don't want it."

"Let me tell you this Kim, when you have come to your senses, this deal is off the table. So think about the irrational decision you are about to make."

I looked around me once more. I think this was going to be the worst decision I will have ever made. I had chosen money over love and failed miserably. I had risked a possibly amazing life in my own comfort zone for this arrogant man who thought he owned me. I messed up, once again. I got it all wrong.

I turned to leave but Hugh grabbed me by the arm and spun me around.

"You better strip off this sexy outfit I bought you and prepare to service me." He sat on the bed, rubbed his crotch and licked his lips as if he actually expected me to obey his orders. Instead, I grabbed a few suitcases and began packing my things. "You are so dramatic. I know you will come running back to me after you leave here. You will soon realize that you are making the biggest mistake of your life."

"You were the biggest mistake of my life. Nothing about this arrangement made me happy." I watched as Hugh's face changed colour. He had the same expression he did prior to hitting me. So I threatened him just in case he had thoughts to repeat the encounter. I told him that if he ever laid hands on me again or tried to stop me from leaving, I would tell his wife everything. This silenced him for a little while, and he resorted to watching me pack. I handed over his car keys, house keys and credit cards. I called a cab then left a few minutes later. I now had possible homelessness to contend with, but I was looking forward to a life without Hugh.

****

"Where is your destination?"

"What?"

"What is the address I am taking you to?"

I didn't know what to tell the cab driver. I didn't think about that. I just knew I wanted to get as far away as possible from Hugh and his apartment. I fought back the tears that were almost clouding my vision. I didn't want to run back to mommy once more. I wasn't sure if Briana was at home or by her man's house, because she was to leave for Italy later today but she was my best bet. I gave the cab driver her address and silently prayed that she was home. I sat quietly for the whole journey reminiscing on my brief encounters with Hugh.

By the time we pulled into Briana's driveway, I was relieved when I saw her vehicle parked. Just to be sure, I told the driver to wait a minute while I check the person on the inside. I knocked on the gate and called her a few times before I saw her peeking through one of the windows. After seeing this, I paid the driver then took my luggage out the car. As Briana opened up her home, her face was plagued with concern. I avoided eye contact with her as I entered her house. I flung myself down on the sofa and waited for her to re arm her house. I watched her as she poured a glass of water from the refrigerator before joining me on the sofa.

222

"So are you all set for Italy?"

"Yes, I think so. I am excited about the trip."

"Steve is taking you places you have never been. Must be nice. You are such a lucky woman."

"I am grateful. So are you going to make me interrogate you as to why you show up at my house at 4 am with suitcases?"

"I called it quits with Hugh. You were right about everything. He gave me everything, but I still wasn't happy. He was controlling and everything you warned me about. I am sorry. I messed up Bri...I am such a loser."

In that instant, the tears flowed, and I couldn't control myself. I bawled.

"Oh Kim, you are so stubborn." Briana said as she came closer and hugged me.

I bawled even more as I nestled my head on her breast, soaking her night gown with my tears. Her hugs were so comforting. She hugged me and became extremely quiet which was unlike her. I looked up at her for a second and realized that she was crying as well. She must have felt my pain. I hugged her even tighter and there was a long moment of silence.

After we both managed to recompose ourselves. She looked at me and asked the million dollar question. "So what now? What is your plan b?

I had no idea. I had nothing in place. I thought I would have lived a rich, happily ever after. I didn't consider these things.

"Going back to mom's house is definitely out of the picture. So that leaves staying with either you or Bugz?"

Briana looked pensive.

"I will be gone for two weeks. Can you honestly promise me that you will stay out of trouble and not burn my house down while I am away?"

I laughed.

"Kim, I am serious? Don't do anything stupid." She said that sternly; I could tell that she was as serious as a judge.

"I promise. I will keep your home safe. Staying here is way better than being homeless."

"While I am gone, you need to do a serious reality check Kim. You can't keep living like this. You need to take life more seriously and focus on achieving long term goals. I am not going down this road again with you Kim, I swear to God. This is your last chance. You need to sort yourself out."

She then proceeded to show me how to operate the security system after which she got dressed. I assisted her with her makeup and we talked for a few more minutes before Steve came to pick her up. I hugged her tightly. I kind of felt like she was leaving me permanently. I had the feeling I would never see her again.

"I miss you already." I said as she pulled the luggage out the door.

"Take care of her," I shouted to Steve before waiving to him.

"Please be safe Kim. Call me if anything ok? I mean anything, doesn't matter what time it is. I love you."

She kissed me on the cheeks then left. I felt the tears well up the moment the car sped off. I was officially all alone.

I locked myself in the house and slept for the rest of the day. I felt very sad, and all I wanted to do was sleep. I was jolted out of my deep slumber several hours after with thoughts of Briana. I wondered where in the world she was, because I knew she had long hours to travel in order to arrive in Italy. She must be drained, but I am sure it will be worth it. It wasn't long before I drifted back to sleep.

21

Briana

Did I mention that I love my life? Well, if I didn't, I love my life. I love everything about it and the people in it. I was in Italy. Can you believe I was staying at a five star resort in Italy? This was my pretty woman moment. I loved Steve and thanked God every day for bringing him into my life. Steve bought me a new dress and a bottle of champagne that he insisted I didn't open. He said he wanted that bottle to take on the trip. Today we were scheduled for a gondola ride in the canals of Venice. I was so excited. Even though we were still a bit jet lagged, more myself than Steve because he was used to all this travelling, we started out early that day nevertheless.

Venice was the first European city that I had ever visited, but I found it to be very romantic, unique and beautiful. I was fascinated by the fact that this city was mostly connected by waterways and bridges. It was an awesome experience for me to be sight-seeing and exploring a city whose mode of commute were gondolas. It was just picture perfect. Along the canal, I had a nice view of the magnificent facades of some of the city's most beautiful buildings. We made brief stops at the side walk cafes where we took advantage of the photo ops of both the architecture and the sea. At this point in time, life was perfect. We walked hand in hand,

and I fought hard to control my emotions. I was bursting with joy at how beautiful everything was.

As we took our seats in the next gondola, I couldn't help but to flood Steve with passionate kisses. I was happy and having a great time, and I needed him to know that. I placed my head on his shoulders and nestled my hands in his. I could no longer hold back my tears. He eased me off his shoulders and wiped my tears. He looked me in the eyes and told me that he loved me. He then continued to tell me that the year and a half that we had been together had been the best time of his live and he couldn't imagine being with anyone else. Of course, his speech only enhanced the wealth of emotions I was already experiencing. He told me that he couldn't wait to spend the rest of his life with me and that he had a question to ask. He reached into his blazer pocket. That's when I realized what was about to happen. He got on one knee in the gondola, opened the box and asked if I would marry him?

By this point, I was crying uncontrollably. I was gasping for air and Steve remained on his knees. The words were unable to come from my mouth. He had to ask if the tears meant it was a yes because I still hadn't answered his question. Of course, it was a yes! He put the ring on my finger and it fit perfectly. I couldn't stop staring at the ring, and he couldn't stop staring at me. He sat back down beside me- his new fiancée. Then I was drawn to clapping, screaming and people shouting congratulations from the neighbouring gondolas. I was so happy, I couldn't wait to share the good news with Kim; my soon to be maid of honour. I can't remember ever being this happy. The rest of the gondola ride was just a blur. Next thing I knew were stepping off the gondola to take some more pictures.

"All that Steve is, is all that I will ever need. Thank you Lord for blessing me. I love my life."

22

Kim

Twenty four hours later, I finally heard from Briana. She settled in and sounded happy. I had to do a video call just so she could be at ease that I still had her house intact. I hadn't done much to be honest. I spent most of the hours sleeping and occasionally getting something to eat. In fact, I only had one meal since she left. I didn't have an appetite. I sunk deeper into my funk, as I thought about how I had messed up my life. I couldn't shake the feeling that there was nothing in my life that made me feel whole. Organizing Wings Fiesta weekly was the only thing that truly made me happy, but then I gave that up because of Hugh's conditions. Now I wasn't sure I would ever be able to bounce back in that department, especially since I was partially homeless. My love life was basically over. It's safe to say that I had no luck with good men or at least I failed to realize when I had a good man- a man like Duane. I should have never let him go. I don't think I will ever find a man who would love me unconditionally.

"I hate my life." The tears hit the pillow as I sobbed out loud. I felt like a big loser. I was tired of getting all the scraps. I just wanted to stay in bed until it was all over, this thing called life. Briana said I should do a reality check but I think I was tired of convincing myself that everything would have been ok. I don't think

I wanted to wake up to another day. I just needed to sleep; that way, I would no longer be a burden to everyone. I needed to talk to someone before I left this world, so I called the one person who I thought could help me make sense of where I had gone wrong in my life. I used Briana's house phone seeing that he had blocked my cell number.

"Hi Duane, Its Kim, I know you don't want to talk to me but please don't hang up?" I begged.

"Why are you calling me?"

"I need to talk to you Duane; you have always reasoned with me, told me the truth and showed me the ropes."

"I am not going back into anything with you Kim. I hope things are working in your favour."

"Nooo. Please don't hang up! I yelled. If I ever meant anything to you, please talk to me one last time. Please Duane?"

He sighed deep and long and sounded annoyed but at least I knew that he was still on the line.

"What do you want Kim?"

"I just want to know why my life is so messed up. I just wanted to hear it from someone who used to love me, where I went wrong and why I am destined to end up alone."

"I don't know Kim" he sighed again.

"Please just tell me the truth Duane."

"Fine." He continued. "Physically you are very appealing but then personality wise, you are desperate. You are materialistic and extremely money hungry. So much so that you don't think logically when figures are involved. With qualities like that, you can't escape attracting one type of men. Those who want nothing but a good time. I loved you, but I was broke, so I wasn't good enough for you. Reality didn't seem to ever be enough for you. You needed to be living your fantasy which was to get rich quick, have a nice house and car and live happily ever after by the snap of the fingers. You don't appreciate little things but I figured maybe being in the house of the Lord, you would have turned from your dirty ways. But then when I noticed you were distancing yourself and you were comfortable with the decision you made, making no effort whatsoever to even attend Sunday services, then that was my cue that I needed to move on. In the initial stages of our relationship, you always stressed how you were not the one for me but it took me awhile to finally accept that you were right.

"I am so sorry Duane."

"Yeah I am sure. Is that all you called for?" he asked sounding anxious to get off the phone."

"Yeah I guess. I want you to know something too. I never stopped loving you."

"Good bye Kim. Have a nice life." He ended the call.

I cried once more. I felt so tired. I couldn't get it together. This life had been too exhausting. I just wanted to sleep and not ever worry about messing up and making the same mistakes again. Bad things were always happening to me. I bawled up the sheets and blew my nose into them. I was starting to feel woozy. I wanted to give Briana one last call but my body wouldn't allow me to. I felt my head growing heavier, so I laid on my back. My time is near. The phone fell from my hands. From a distance, I heard someone yelling my name, but it was coming through a tunnel or something. The bottle of pills fell out of my hand. I watched it rolled a few feet but I felt too exhausted to pick it up. I was so tired of hurting that I had fixed it so that it would never happen again. That feeling of calm slowly came over me. I felt my body going numb. My vision blurred, it was happening at any moment. Good bye world.

www.ingramcontent.com/pod-product-compliance
Lightning Source LLC
Chambersburg PA
CBHW071324250626
47159CB00004B/1450